SWITCHBOARD

SWITCHBOARD

by

ROGER LONGRIGG

faber and faber

This edition first published in 2008
by Faber and Faber Ltd
3 Queen Square, London WC1N 3AU

A CIP record for this book is available from the British Library

ISBN 978-0-571-24265-8

To P.

Wrong not, sweet empress of my heart,
The merit of true passion,
With thinking that he feels no smart
Who sues for no compassion.

Sir Walter Raleigh

PART ONE

Autumn on Everest

Chapter One

✣

I was having an affair at the time with a girl named Sue. This ought to have nothing to do with the story. In fact, there ought to be no story. But on that warm September night some high string-holder yawned on his cloudy mountain; twitched his wooden criss-crosses; grinned; and started us all on the steps of our disastrous dance. For on that night I met Perkins. I met Perkins because I was in Sue's bedroom. This was because I was her lover. I don't know why this was, but it's the one good thing about the whole deplorable business.

Sue lived in one of those high, rickety squares in the area that calls itself Chelsea but seems to be Fulham. My relationship with her was not at the time very serious, and was daily becoming less so. A month before I had been climbing her eighty creaking stairs as often as three times a week; now it was more like once in ten days. And those stairs—heavens, those eighty stairs! They were thickly populated even in the small hours. A grey woman in a grey shawl used to stand mewing near the front door; a yellow-eyed man in an army greatcoat dribbled ash from his cigarette to or from the lavatory on the first mezzanine; a plump blonde girl with tartan trousers used to telephone, endlessly, on the third-floor landing; a small, sad Jewish couple carried their pram slowly and very quietly up to the fourth floor. These were the regulars, nesting there. Migrants often appeared, too, singly or in shrill flocks.

The carpet on those stairs went striding up the first two flights, climbing vigorously between the off-white walls and the pitch-pine banisters; but at the second floor it began to lose heart, developing bare patches and long, mysterious stains. At the third floor, just under the telephone, it gave up: one ascended beyond that point on dark, spongy wood dappled into a schoolroom irregularity.

Sue's floor seemed an afterthought. The stairs changed direction and paled to buff before they reached it, as though they could hardly take seriously anyone's intention to get that far; even Sue's door had an improvised look, being small, and only fairly rectangular, and bearing in its midst a brass knocker in the form of a ship sweeping towards one under all plain sail.

I spent many, many happy hours at the end of that improbable rainbow. Sue was a part-time actress who lived on a small allowance from her remote family—a little fair girl, thin, and unemphatically beautiful. She had a rare and satisfying shamelessness, and though intelligent liked not talking. Her flat was only a flat by courtesy. It consisted of one largeish room (the bed was barely disguised as a sofa) and a small bathroom-kitchen. There were no curtains on the windows, and the minimum of carpet, and a gas fire, but it was quite comfortable. *We* were quite comfortable. All the same, I was feeling—not exactly restive, but as one feels when a tune one knows is shaping steadily towards its final cadence. Besides, I did not want Sue to get too dependent on me, or indeed me on her.

The evening I am talking about—the evening this story starts—I had the pre-cadence feeling quite strongly. At the same time I was enjoying Sue's uncomplicated immodesty as much as ever. I was sitting on the window-seat (there was a kind of window-seat) watching her prepare herself gradually for bed. This was always quite a performance, and always different. Presently she went out into the kitchen to get the coffee she had been making, and I allowed my eyes to wander out of the window. I had never thought of the world outside that window as being anything but the thin ether surrounding a great height: but in fact a row of equally tall houses showed us their irregular backs, divided from the houses of Sue's square only by small, scraggy gardens. I looked at them without interest. A few windows showed as yellow, orange, or dark red squares haphazardly placed on the flat curtain of the darkness. A few chimneys pointed haphazardly at the invisible stars. A minor crash and a woman's clear laugh rang suddenly across the chasm. A car went noisily from left to right in the street beyond, changing gear at the corner and then fading into silence along the Fulham Road.

Sue called from the kitchen: "Eddie."

"Hullo?"

"Ready."

"Oh good."

I rose and joined her, and she put a large cup of coffee into my hand. We went back into the main room together and sat side by side on the bed, sipping and smoking. It was a warm, still evening; though neither of us had anything on we were no more than pleasantly cool. The coffee was hot and black and strong. All was extremely well. Sue got up and moved vaguely about the room, tidying. I watched her with pleasure. She took an ashtray from the mantelpiece and emptied it into the waste-paper basket; then plumped out a cushion on the armchair; then picked up an ashtray I had left on the floor by the window-seat. As she straightened her back she glanced out of the window. Something seemed to hold her for a second. Then, to my surprise, she dropped back to the floor.

11

"Eddie—— "

"What on earth are you doing?"

"Turn the light off."

"All right."

I walked over to the door and snapped off the switch. The room seemed impenetrably black at first, but after a second or two I saw Sue's pale back bending over the sill, and then other objects crept into faint visibility in the light from the windows opposite.

"Look," whispered Sue, "the window bang opposite."

"Which one?" I said, "the unlit one?"

"Yes. I'm sure there's someone there."

"Well, probably."

"Yes, but I mean watching us."

"*What?*"

"*Look*. Did you see that? A kind of glint, moving."

"Yes. Yes—golly."

"Field-glasses or something."

"Could be, yes. Golly. Do you mind frightfully?"

"Well," she said, "no. But it is rather awful—— "

"Which floor is he on—fourth? No, fifth. And it's the second house from the corner. Hm."

"If I stay and put on a show—— "

"Put on a *show?*"

"*—in* my dressing-gown. . . . I'll pretend you're still here—— "

"Yes! I'll go and sort him out. I hope he's not enormous. Where are my clothes? Not that I need many of them. . . ."

Eight minutes later I was standing outside the spy's house. It was quite dark this side. I wondered which his number was, and I inspected by the light of a match the names by the vertical row of bells. About 5, it would be. 5 *Ostrogoth*, I read. 6 *Perkins*. 4 *Coote*. After a dubious moment I rang 5. There was a long pause. An old man crossed the street with an old dog on a lead. "Come on, damn you," he said. "Come on, blast you." Come on, damn you, I thought. Come on, blast you.

Eventually the door opened a very short way.

"Yais?"

I had not rehearsed this part. "Er, Mrs. Ostrogoth?"

"Yais."

"Er, do your windows face out this way? Or to the back? Because—— "

"Who are you, eh? Vat do you vant?"

"Well, you see, I live opposite, at the back, and my windows face the back of this house, and—— "

"So?"

"Yes. And I was looking, just now, out of the window, and—— "

"So?"

"Yes, and my wife—— "

"You ring my bell at ziss time to esk qvastion about vindow—— "

"Ha ha, yes, it must seem odd, but my wife—— "

She slammed the door.

After a pause I tried 4 *Coote*; almost at once the door opened and a cheery face peered out.

"Ha! Good! Another recruit! Come along old boy, very glad to see you, up this way—I'll go first, shall I?—who sent you, Billie?"

"Er—— "

"That girl's a marvel, absolute marvel, where she finds you all from I can't think—well, I don't mean it *that* way, ha ha—personally I don't mind telling you I've had terrible trouble, terrible. Hours on the phone and *arguments*, God. Talk about slow-witted. Talk about *thick*. People astound me, they really do, here's a chance to make quids and *quids* and what do they say—well, they say, *well*, they don't really

13

ap*prove*, they've been caught b*efore*, you never heard such crap. Well. Here we are, go straight in, I expect you know everybody. Beer? Or, wait a minute, I think there may be a bit of whisky left, hang on a moment, I'll just go and have a peer, hang on, shan't be a mo'."

The room faced the front, away from Sue's window. It was dark and crowded, and a lot of strange people were discussing something.

"If you're Frank's child, whose child is Maggie?"

"*I'm* Maggie's child, one of them, I don't know who the other is, in fact I'm not sure there *is* one—— "

"Oh *dear*, now Maggie's let us down—— "

"And in that case who's Frank's child?"

"Maggie."

"Oh—— "

"Ah," said an American girl with bat-wing glasses, "here's someone. Whose child are *you?*"

"What?" I was baffled.

"Or are you a spare?"

"Completely spare."

"Goody. We can surely do with some spares. We better fit you in under Maggie, I think. Now, have you got your copy of the rules?"

"Rules?"

"Yes, of course," she said impatiently, "you don't think we could run a thing like this without *rules*, do you? I don't have so many copies left but I better give you one."

"Oh—thanks. . . ."

"See you give your children copies. That's a *must*"

"I haven't got any children."

"Of course you don't have any children *yet*. You only *joined* this evening. You have to get children tomorrow, and bring them tomorrow evening to—well, it's all in the rules. Now I guess this'll be your chart."

14

"Chart? Er, *chart?*"

"Sure. How'd you think we'd get along without the chart?"

"I don't know."

"You bet you don't."

"Here you are, old boy," said the jovial man, reappearing but of the gloom. "Best I could do."

I sipped the glass of cider and looked round.

"Well, if Frank goes in *here,*" said a young man with a huge sheet of paper, strangely inscribed, spread out in front of him, "if Frank fits in *here,* what do we do about this gap?"

"No, no. Frank goes in *here.* See? *Maggie* fits in this gap."

"No I don't. I fit in this gap."

"No no. The *other* Maggie."

"Oh—well, this side's a day late."

"No, *this* side's a day *early.*"

"Oh—— "

"Have you paid your half-crown?" said the spectacled girl.

"Half-crown? My *half-crown?*"

"Yeah. Your children pay tomorrow, to whoever's peak of the mountain then."

"I'm sorry, I just don't understand any of this."

"*Lis*ten, it's *sim*ple. Tomorrow you go to today's next-to-top's party, because tomorrow he'll be top, see? Peak, I mean. Of your mountain. Your children pay their half-crowns to him, so he gets a pound altogether, and he sends it to the Everest of the day, whoever that is, er, it's on the chart, look—— "

"Oh," the light broke, "I *see.* This is one of those chain-letter things."

"No, it is nut *eether* a chain letter. Well, I guess it's the same idea. Only it's people instead of letters, so it's quicker and you can *reely* check up, see, as you go. You want to, too—hi, Fred, no I mean *Ferd,* where's the chart?—look, you're here, and that means—— "

"Fascinating," a tubby pink-faced man was saying in an excited cockney voice, "*fascinating*. It was like the courtship of two great pink birds. Gosh! It'll make a wonderful chapter in—what?"

"Perkins," someone repeated, "where are *your* children?"

"They're a bit late—— "

"They surely are," said the American girl. "Are they definitely coming?"

"Well. . . ."

"Oh Perkins!"

"Well, I tell you what, I'll make *jolly* sure they come tomorrow with *their* children. That's just as good."

"Ye-es."

"*Well* as I was saying, just like two huge flamingoes or something, it was really balletic, passing across the window, brilliantly lit—hand of a master, you'd have said—*gosh*, talk about courtship rites—talk about *The Golden Bough*—talk about symbolical movement—talk about. . . ."

"Don't, Perkins. Just don't talk about anything for a bit. Now Ferdie, if this corner's all right we can afford to throw all our spares in here, under Maggie, where it's weakest—— "

"Here," I said, "you. *I'm* interested. Will you show me?"

The pink face, a foot below mine, took on a dubious look. I had never before seen a face change expression so totally, so suddenly; those broad shiny features became joke-dubious, ham-actor dubious. It was like the villain in a silent film turning aside to sneer. I couldn't believe it was real.

"*Well,*" he said, "it's not quite decent, you know, to show anyone a thing like that—— "

"You looked," I said.

"Ah, that's different, quite different. I'm an artist. I've got to observe. For the painter, his nude model. For me, Life. It's clinical with me, you see. It's dispassionate. I'm just a recording machine. I'm just—— "

"A camera," I murmured.

"Yes, in a manner of speaking, yes. Well. You see, I don't think I *can*—— "

"Listen," I lied, "I'm a poet. I have to have—— "

"Oh *well*, then. . . . No, I'm sorry—— "

"Oh come on," I said impatiently, "which window?"

"Oh *well*, my flat, up here."

I edged after him past the clamouring group round the chart ("Billie's great-grandchild fits *here*"—"No, no, that's Maggie's parents *there*") and followed his short back up some dingy stairs.

"Here we are. My garret. My eyrie on the world. . . . Ah, they've put the light on. Look, there she is. Oh, what a pity, she's put a dressing-gown on, I wonder why? Now that might be *very* interesting. A false-modesty stage is part of the rite, do you think? *Very* interesting. I wonder where *he's* got to. In bed, I expect. Now that's very odd, very odd, most interesting—what wouldn't I give for an enormous periscope—— "

The room was dark, and had an indefinable sweet smell. On the sill of the open window, clearly visible in the light from the brilliant rectangle opposite, lay a huge pair of naval field-glasses. Into the rectangle, as I watched, swam Sue in her blue cotton dressing-gown. She was apparently talking to someone invisible; her face wore a vivaciously conversational expression quite foreign to her tranquil nature.

"Yes," I said, "yes I see. Pity he's hiding."

"He's in bed—that's how I read it," said Perkins judiciously. "Lying in bed *panting*—that's how I read it. Now what I'd like to know is, is he panting more or less because she's put her dressing-gown on?"

"Less," I said, because I knew that's what Perkins wanted me to say.

"No. More! And I'll tell you why—— "

I suddenly got bored. "Listen. I happen to be the man she's talking to."

"Ha ha—er, what do you mean? You can't be. You're *here*."

"That's right. She's acting for you."

Perkins rushed over to the door and switched the light on. On his face as he stared at me was a ludicrously exaggerated expression of astonishment. "*Gosh!*" Then in a flash astonishment gave way (as in a baby, as in a savage) to terror. "You've come over here to find me—to *beard* me—— "

"Yes. And what I've *actually* come over here to do is—— "

His magic-lantern face changed its slide again, and I was suddenly impressed. Its new expression was dignity. "Now—" he held up a podgy hand, "now now. Interests of pure research. Interests of art. Don't be small about—— "

"My God," I said, "you have got a nerve."

"I have the courage of my convictions," he said soberly. "You may strike me. You may bludgeon me. You may lash me with your tongue—— "

"I haven't yet decided *what* to lash you with—— "

"—but you will never rout me from my last bloody ditch. (I'm not using bloody as a swear-word, you understand. Actual blood about, I mean)—— "

"Yes, that's what I'm coming to—— "

"I shall feel proud," he said, "proud. Proud of my bruises of body or spirit. Or *both*. I shall have been a martyr in—— "

"Oh Christ, shut up. Is this true? Are you writing a book on sex or something?"

"Not only sex. Life. Partly sex, of course, because as I always say—— "

"Oh, sort of philosophical?"

"Indeed yes. A philosophical novel. A panorama of contemporary life. An attempt to—— "

"Far advanced, is it?"

"Well, half way. I've written about 200,000 words so far."

"Quite a long book," I said.

"Long, yes. But alas! all too short for its mighty subject. Too short for—— "

"Yes, yes. I'm assuming, generously as*sum*ing, that you're telling the truth. So I shan't on this occasion, er, take any action. I don't know why. But if I ever catch you—if I so much as *glimpse*—— "

"Are you going back, now?"

"Yes."

"Good. Because you see I shall be most interested to see how this interruption has affected the pattern of your behaviour when you join—— "

"Look, I've just told you—— "

"Yes, but don't you feel you *ought* to complete my knowledge of this most interesting manifestation of contemporary—— "

"No."

"Oh," he said stiffly, "well. I see."

"And I warn you, Perkins—— "

"I can't persuade you to reconsider?"

"*Blast* you, I—— "

"Think what the world may be missing. Think what you're stealing, really, from your own grandchildren—— "

"*Damn* you, I—— "

"Well, if you're adamant, perhaps you'll just *tell* me what you're going to do—oh, very well. I must leave posterity an incomplete picture. Posterity will judge our generation on incomplete—— " He was quite angry. "Good-bye," he said, more stiffly than ever. "I think you'd better go now."

I left, astounded, and started down the murky stairs.

"No no, let's start again," I heard through the jovial man's door. "Let's for God's sake get this straight. If

Perkins and Maggie get the four grandchildren they need—— "

"Eight."

"Four *each*. And this new chap gets his—— "

"He doesn't get *grand*children. Not yet. Why do you say he's got to get *grand*children?"

"Children I mean, for God's sake—— "

I passed on down the stairs.

Two minutes later I was using my key on the front door of Sue's house, and after a climb that seemed more exhausting than usual I was back on Sue's bed asking for another cup of coffee.

"*Well*?" she said.

I told her the story.

"*God*. Did he show you the book?"

"No. Oh no. I wish I'd thought of that."

"Well. What a thing. What's that in your hand?"

I looked down. I held, clasping them like a talisman, the papers the American girl had insisted on my taking. "Oh. I'd forgotten these. Some kind of chart. And—I say, listen to this:

The Everest Club (I read)

If you and your descendants fulfil all your obligations, you can make £128 for the investment of only 2s. 6d. This is the purpose of the Everest Club.

The procedure is as follows.

When you join the club you do so as someone's child. You pay 2s. 6d. to the peak of your particular mountain, of the base of which you personally form one-eighth. You must now get two children for yourself—ones who you think will perform their obligations properly—and take them to the peak-party of the new peak of your mountain. They pay 2s. 6d. each to the peak. You yourself move at this stage one step up towards the peak of your mountain, and your

*children now form one-quarter of its base. This is the second evening.
On your third evening your children will each introduce two children
at the peak-party of the new peak of your mountain. You now
move a further step towards the peak. Your grandchildren, of course,
now form one-half of the base of your mountain. On the following
evening—your fourth—your four grandchildren will each bring two
great-grandchildren to your peak-party. Your descendants now
number eight: you are therefore at the head of your own mountain.
You collect eight 2s. 6d.s from your eight new descendants, and you
send this £1 to the Everest of the evening. You will be one of 128
people doing so. On your fifth to tenth evenings you have no actual
obligations, but you are advised to keep as close a check as possible on
the way your Everest is developing, since, obviously, if one of your
children breaks down you cannot get more than £64, and so to a
proportionately lesser extent for your more remote descendants. On
your eleventh evening, if your Everest is complete, 128 of your
descendants will be giving peak-parties, each to eight great-grandchildren; they will each collect eight 2s. 6d.s which they will bring or
send to you. You will therefore collect £128.*

*Make two copies of these rules and give them to your children.
Make sure they make copies and give them to their children. It is
vital that the rules should be kept, or the whole thing will break down.*

*When you give your peak-party, on your fourth evening, give each
of your great-grandchildren a chart like the one you have been given
this evening, showing them where they fit into your mountain and
giving the names and addresses of the other people in the mountain.
This is necessary in order to tell them where to take their children
to on the following evening, and where to send their peak-party
money to on their fourth evenings; it will also help them put their
own descendants into the picture.*

Good luck!

"Well! What about that?"
"How on earth did you get it?"

"Well, that's how I found Perkins."

"What, at a peak-party?"

"Yes, it must have been. They thought I was a recruit. I got kind of sucked in—— "

"Did you pay half a crown?"

"Come to think of it I didn't."

"Have you got the chart? Oh yes, let's see. . . ."

The chart looked like a family tree. The name Coote was at the top—the peak of the mountain. The jovial fellow who gave me the cider, no doubt. Perkins was in one of the four spaces one step from the bottom. Clearly, I fitted into one of the eight great-grandchildren spaces, but I had no idea which. Tomorrow I was supposed to take two people to someone else's party—one of the two names immediately below Coote. Then events were to march grandly towards the apotheosis of my being given £128.

"This sounds rather a good idea," I said.

"Yes, we must certainly do it. I'll be one of your children."

"All right. I'll get another somewhere. . . . The thing is, I don't know where I fit in on this chart."

"On the bottom."

"Yes, but where?"

"It doesn't matter."

"Yes it does. If I'm *here*," I pointed to the left-hand side of the chart, "we go to this Frankie person in Tedworth Square tomorrow night, because he—— "

"Or she."

"Or she, yes, he or she will be the new peak of this side. But if I'm *here* we go to Billie, you see, in Bayswater."

"Billie in Bayswater. Sounds like a song. Yes, I see. Difficult."

"Children you can trust to fulfil their obligations, it says. Yes, I can see that. Can I trust you, darling?"

"You *know* you can. Look, what I don't understand is,

when we get to the top do we have to wait in an enormous queue?"

"No, that's the whole point."

"I don't get it. Every day your chances of actually being the person being paid off are halved."

"No, they're exactly the same."

"But there are more and more people at the bottom, and there's only one—what's it called?—Everest."

"No. On any one evening there can be as many Everests as you like. As there happen to *be*, I mean. Each mountain splits down the middle each day, you see. Tomorrow this one will be two mountains, each with eight new people at the bottom, with these two people as peaks. Two peaks today where one was yesterday. The next evening there'll be four. These four here—this evening's peak's grandchildren. See?"

"Ye-es. What it is to be a statistician, darling. But look—at this moment there are at least 128 potential Everests all over London——"

"In theory, yes. At least that many. Actually, only that *few* if the chap at the very top today, the Everest, actually started the thing himself."

"Yes. Hm." She frowned. "Eleven days from now, in theory, you'll be one of at least 128 people, each with 128 people under you, each with eight people under *them* all clutching half-crowns. . . ."

"Yes. . . . Put like that——"

"In a couple of weeks it'll involve the whole *world*——"

"Yes——"

"Well. Even so, I think we ought to try. Obviously it depends on getting in early enough. I wonder if we have? Half a crown's not much to risk, and I could use £128, I must say. . . . Have some more coffee and let's go to bed."

"Good idea."

Chapter Two

✢

H"ere's all the Belgravia material, Mr. Melot."
"Thank you," I said.
Jacqueline, my efficient but complicated secretary, put a formidable pile of papers on my desk. Before she allowed her hands to leave them she twitched them fussily into a symmetrical stack. I was reminded of a dog-handler I had once seen, showing a terrier at a local show: he had pushed the poor creature's legs about, hauled tightly on its lead, forced it into a position of awkward, unnatural correctness which seemed to me quite irrelevant to the dog's real qualities. I didn't care whether the Belgravia papers were stacked like a new pack of cards or not: they would provide me with exactly the same information tidy or untidy. But I couldn't say this to Jacqueline.

"Ah," I said heartily, "thanks."

She picked up three paper-clips from the small clear space on my desk by the inside telephone, and put them in the pocket of her smart, unbecoming black dress. Then, with an infinitely slight, infinitely irritating sigh she used the side of her mauve right hand to sweep some cigarette ash from the other clear space on the desk, by the outside telephone. As she walked away she wiped her hand on the seat of her dress, leaving a faint but perceptible grey shadow on the wool. She closed the door in a soft, grieved way, and I applied myself with something like relief to the dreary task in front of me.

It was ten-thirty of the morning after my first peak-party.

The papers Jacqueline had given me were the results of some market research we had done into consumer buying habits in the writing-paper field: and I was soon deep in what seemed (since I had had a late night) quite meaningless percentages. I began to make notes for my report. "43 per cent of the sample preferred ruled paper to plain, but 92 per cent of this 43 per cent could give no reason for their preference," I wrote. I could give an excellent reason for their preference, but I would have to look into the class breakdown of that 43 per cent. "86 per cent of the sample preferred blue paper to any other colour. 29 per cent of this 86 per cent preferred dark blue, 18 per cent azure, and the remaining 53 per cent middle-to-light blue. This appears to show conclusively—— " Well, that was easy. "The ¼ per cent who preferred black paper and white ink—— " That was easier still.

At twelve o'clock the telephone rang.

"Eddie?" said the Chairman's voice.

"Speaking. Is that you, Jonathan?"

"Yes. Look, are you frightfully tied up?"

"Well, all the Belgravia Bond stuff has just come in, but—— "

"God, yes I see. Well, I wonder if you could possibly spare me a minute or two? I'm frightfully sorry to bother you when you've got all that on your plate. There's no *special* hurry, but—— "

"I'll come now."

"Thanks awfully, Eddie."

That was one of the things I liked about Jonathan Cornish. Although I was the head of a department, there can't have been a second's doubt in his mind that I'd come within a minute of his call. I stood in that sort of relationship to him. All his employees did. All the same, he would never dream of asking me to come except as a favour, or, when I had come, of talking to me except as to an expert whom he was grateful to have the chance of consulting. I stood in *that* sort of relationship to him. All his employees did. He was a man of great talents, and this was his greatest. It was not, I suppose, *completely* unconscious, but this was as far as you could go in the direction of saying that he turned on the charm. He had a remarkable capacity for arousing loyalty. He certainly aroused mine.

For all these reasons, as soon as I had put my inside telephone back on its hook I rose and left my room.

I had, unfortunately, to pass Jacqueline's desk on my way to the main corridor and Jonathan, just as other people had, fortunately, to pass her on their way to me.

"Oh; Jacqueline," I said.

She stopped typing with the air of a musician interrupted half a bar before a climax. "Yes, Mr. Melot?"

"I've left a lot of papers all over my desk. Could you please see that no one disturbs them at all? I'm just off to see the Chairman."

"Very well, Mr. Melot."

I walked down the corridor and into Jonathan's ante-room. His secretary—a large, spectacular girl almost as intelligent as she thought she was—stood placing gladioli in orthodox disarray in a tall blue vase.

"Oh, hullo Eddie. Do you like them like this?"

"Morning, Lavinia. Yes, very much."

"They're boring flowers, but something *can* be done with them."

"Yes, indeed."

"Shall I tell Mr. Cornish you're here?"

"No, don't bother. He's expecting me,"

"Oh, good. Well—— " She put a purple cabbage-leaf and two dead sticks like small lavatory brushes among her gladioli, and stepped back to examine the effect. These additions increased the orthodoxy of the arrangment almost to night-club point, but she seemed pleased.

I went through into Jonathan's room.

"Ah, Eddie, hullo. I *am* sorry to drag you here like this—— "

"Hullo Jonathan. No, not a bit."

"Do sit down. Cigarette?" As he leant forward, the china box in his outstretched hand, a thing happened typical of the things that were always happening to Jonathan. The sun, hidden until that moment behind a black fast-moving cloud, came out with theatrical suddenness, flooding into the big room with theatrical brilliance to light Jonathan's head from behind. His thick, straight grey hair was edged with a golden line; a small wash of gold ran from his ear to a deep furrow beside his mouth. He looked preposterously magnificent. I once saw Magdalen tower in exact profile when they turned the floodlights on: but it wasn't quite like that because the effect then had been of tower-shaped, highly polished filigree with no masonry in the middle. I once saw the first night of a new production of *Tristan* at Covent Garden in which, near the end of the second act, they accidentally turned on a spotlight exactly behind King Mark. It *was* like that. Than which, it now occurs to me, nothing could be more ironic.

When I had taken a cigarette, and lit his and then mine, he leant back, blowing a cloud of smoke up into the broken shaft of sunlight.

"Eddie, do you know a chap called Christopher Townsend? He might just have overlapped you at Oxford."

"Yes, I remember him very well."

"He must be younger than you?"

27

"Yes. He came up my last year. He was at the House. Big fair man. He had an enormous car and he hunted and went up to London a lot—— " A Bullingdon man; the golden boy of a set I profoundly did not belong to for at least eight excellent reasons.

"Did you like him?"

"Yes," I said truthfully, "very much." His charm, his intelligence, his immediate and surprising sympathy with men totally unlike himself—Oh yes, I had liked and admired and envied him enormously.

"Good. He's my godson, you know."

"*Is* he? No, I didn't know—— "

"Yes. After he went down—five years ago, that would be—he went to the States—— "

"Yes, I heard from him once or twice." A postcard from New York (Times Square at night); a comic postcard from Los Angeles ("How many times do I gotta tell ya, Junior, that spittoon is fer *spittin'* in!").

"Oh—you knew him well, then?"

"No, not really. . . ." Dinner at my college, dinner in Woodstock, an afternoon at a cricket match, an evening in a punt with some girls.

"Well, he's been working in New York for the last three years in the Television Department of a big agency."

"Which one?"

Jonathan told me. I was impressed.

"It's supposed to be the best television agency in the States—— "

"And therefore the world."

"And therefore, as you say, the world. Anyhow, he's come home, and he wants a job, and I thought I'd give him one. What do you think?"

"Yes," I said enthusiastically. "That's excellent news. With that background he'd be exactly what we want."

"That's how it struck me. From the television point of view alone his experience would be worth any amount to us just now."

The Act setting up the Independent Television Authority had recently gone through Parliament, and firms like ourselves were in a state of continuous excitement about it.

"*Exactly* what we need," I said.

"Yes. And it's not just that. I'm very likely biased, I mean I've known him all his life and so on, but he's always seemed to me a remarkably talented chap."

"I quite agree."

"And finally there's this. I'm telling you all this, Eddie, because we know each other so well, and also because it concerns you. I know you won't let it go any farther—— "

"No. No, of course not."

"Christopher is my heir."

"Ah. Yes, I see."

"That proposition may have, er, riders here or it may not, we can't possibly tell. Very likely not. But I hope it does."

"So do I."

"Do you really, Eddie? I am glad. Of course, he may not want to stay here, or even stay in the business. And as far as you're concerned, you may want to move any moment—— "

"I hardly think so."

Jonathan smiled. "Well, good. Now, are you doing anything for lunch, Eddie?"

"No."

"I said I'd give Christopher lunch at the club. It would be very nice if you'd come too, if you'd like to?"

"I'd love to, but—— "

"Oh, it isn't a great godfather-godson reunion—don't be restrained by that thought. He's been home a fortnight now, and he's been staying at Fordings. We've had all the reunion stuff. Besides, even if we hadn't—— " He left it un-finished, but it made me feel very pleased.

"Oh well then, of course I'll come, thank you."

"Fine. I'll pick you up in half an hour."

"Right."

As I went past Lavinia's desk she looked up from Sir Kenneth Clark's *Landscape into Art* to give me one of her smiles. Her flowers stood on the oval table above the new, carefully haphazard *Tatlers, Vogues,* and *New Yorkers.* They went well with the *Tatlers* and *Vogues*; not so well with the *New Yorkers.*

"Very nice," I said.

"Thank you, Eddie, do you really think so? I must say I think—— "

I felt pleased about Christopher Townsend, and also about lunch, and therefore I felt strong: but not strong enough for a conversation about flower arrangement with Lavinia, and above all not strong enough for a conversation about Piero della Francesca with Lavinia. So I grunted and went back to Belgravia Bond.

As soon as I saw my desk I rang for Jacqueline.

"Yes, Mr. Melot?"

"Who's been mucking about with my papers?"

"No one," she said indignantly, "naturally. I tidied up myself, that's all, and *no one*—— "

"I distinctly told you, Jacqueline, that these papers were not to be disturbed. I left them in exactly the order I wanted them to be in when I came back. Will you *kindly*, in future, restrain your damned passion for neatness when I go to the trouble of telling—— "

"I beg your pardon, Mr. Melot," she said stiffly. "I'm very sorry. You'll see that the papers are all in their correct order—— "

"Listen, Jacqueline. These are figures, tables, graphs,

cross-references—all sorts of things. I have to look at several papers at a time to make one note. I can't work at all unless they're spread out exactly as I want them spread out. Will you *please* get it into your head once and for all that when I particularly *say*—"

What I ought to have anticipated would happen happened: she burst into tears.

"I'm sorry," she moaned, "I'm derribly sorry. I try to please you. It seemed (sniff) *criminal* to leave all your papers strewn about like that. I just had to make them neat for you when you came back. I thought you'd be *pleased* to find them all tidy and looking nice. Instead you're (hic) *angry*—"

"I'm sure you did it for the best, Jacqueline," I said desperately, "I know you meant to be kind. But I'd really be much more pleased if you'd—"

A storm of sobbing drowned my words even in my own ears. "Oo oo oo. You just don't *like* me, that's all; I'm not pretty, I know, but I do *try*. . . . I don't know why you don't *sack* me—"

"Nonsense, Jacqueline. I like you very much and I wouldn't dream of sacking you. You're far too efficient—I don't know how this department would manage without you. I depend on you more than you realize—"

"Oo oo," she sobbed, "hic *oo*."

"Besides," I ploughed on, "I'm always very touched by the trouble you take, I really do notice it and appreciate it, believe me, like sweeping up the cigarette ash I *clumsily* drop on my desk, as you did this morning—"

"Oo—you're just saying that to—"

I fought a terrible battle against almost ungovernable irritation. Jonathan could have dealt with this beautifully. Come to think of it, so could Perkins. I was useless at it.

"Now calm down, Jacqueline," I said soothingly, "calm down, there's a good girl—"

"*Girl*," she shrieked, "ha ha—— " Her awkward, chicly covered shoulders shook and shuddered.

"Certainly," I said, "certainly you're a girl. Why, my goodness, you don't look—— "

It is frightful to think—and I thought it all the time in her presence—that the only reason I didn't sack Jacqueline was because I hadn't the courage to face the scene there'd be.

Fourteen minutes after this deplorable episode I was washing my hands in the well-equipped cloak-room of Grey's. It was a soothing and splendid process. Hot water rushed out of an enormous brass tap into the enormous white basin—one of a dozen let into the brawn-like slab of marble that runs the length of one side of the room—and I made my choice from among the several available tablets of good, unluxurious soap. I had three alternative nail-brushes, all as old, tried, and respectable as the pair of hair-brushes in the downstairs lavatory of a country house, and all alas! as ineffective: none of them shifted the last stubborn half-millimetre of office grime from under my fingernails. Two pieces of pumice-stone offered themselves; with both I scrubbed with more hope than usual at the faint, horrible yellowness of my fore and middle fingers.

After this agreeable cleansing I addressed myself to the less pleasant task of brushing my hair. Christopher once said I had hearty hair; I saw what he meant. It sticks up, irremediably, in rugger-player's ridges. If ever I wanted to look smooth (and I suppose I one day might) my beastly hair would make all my efforts laughable. So, come to think of it, would my beastly face, which I have disliked as long as I can remember. It is one of those broad faces. It goes red whenever I am hot, cold, embarrassed, happy, or drunk. It is fairly red even when my temperature and pulse-rate are normal. Christopher called it an Anglican face. I loathed it.

Glancing at Jonathan's reflection (he was washing his hands in the next-door basin to mine) I wondered how it would feel to know you looked distinguished and elegant and clever and honest. Altering focus, I watched the reflection of the cloak-room servant, a stooped silver man like a film prime minister. Despondently I looked back at my own wholesome mug and tried to flatten my Twickenham hair with a soft, long-handled brush.

Suddenly another head appeared beside mine in the glass: a big fair head with tight brown skin and a wide, widely-grinning mouth.

I spun round. "Christopher!"

"My dear old Major, how are you?"

"Very well. How *very* good to see you."

"And you. Think of your working for Uncle Jonathan."

"Think of *your* doing so, Christopher," said Jonathan.

"Am I to?"

"Yes, if you like the idea."

"I like it very much," said Christopher. "Very much indeed. I've been hoping for days you'd say that."

"Well, I had to consult Eddie."

"You gave your consent, Major?"

"Well," I said, "a long probationary period, of course, at a nominal salary, and then some intensive training in the Despatch Department—— "

"Then WOSB, hm?"

"We-ell—— "

"Ha!" he buffeted me on the shoulder, "It's splendid to find yon here, Major. Splendid. Great luck, quite unlooked-for. Made my day. I must wash my hands." He turned to the basin.

"What's all this Major stuff?" said Jonathan.

"I've never been able to think of Eddie as anything but a major," said Christopher. "He *must* be a major. Did you ever see anyone who looked so much like a major? Brown boots, that's what he ought to be wearing. Map cases all over him. A battle-bowler, as he would doubtless call it. Whereas you, Uncle Jonathan— "

"Yes?"

"You are, of course, the much-decorated general commanding the minuscule army, with purely ceremonial duties, of a very nice, very silly Margrave in the year 1765."

"Yes," said Jonathan, staring at himself dubiously in the glass, "yes. I'm afraid I see what you mean."

"And I— "

"You, Christopher," I said, "are the popular and dashing Captain Townsend of The Guards, toast of the corporals' wives, delight of chaperons, with whom you are particularly successful, cynosure of all eyes as you sweep into ballrooms on the arm— "

"Where did you learn words like that?" asked Christopher, "and fluency like that? You couldn't have said those things when I knew you."

"Ah. I'm in advertising."

"True," he said, "true. And what a surprise it is. Major Edwin Melot, pride of the Royal Indian Army Ordinance Corps— "

"Come on," said Jonathan, "I want my sherry."

As we went out, two elderly members with purple faces and beautifully polished shoes were hanging their bowlers on pegs.

"R.I.A.O.C.," said one. "Hear that, Puffy? Chap's in the R.I.A.O.C"

"God," said the other, "the chaps some chaps ask here— "

"Though come to think of it," said the first, "I shouldn't have thought there still *was* an R.I.A.O.C. No Indian Army, now, I mean, dammit."

"No. Most extraordinary. Wonder what he's really in. The *chaps* some chaps ask here—— "

We sat near a window in the famous L-shaped dining-room and ate potted shrimps and roast lamb. Christopher did most of the talking, as always. He recounted with prodigious vim some of his odder experiences in New York, making it appear that he had been an unremitting figure of fun, a constantly humiliated blunderer and Aunt Sally, over whom practically the whole metropolitan population had, at one time or another, poured either scorn or cold, soapy water.

"—I found I couldn't pay," he was finishing one story. "They were most put out."

"What did they do? Put *you* out?"

"Not at once. I pretended I was French and knew no English. So they immediately produced a French waiter. '*Ah, monsieur, vous êtes Français. Il faut vous expliquer que*—— '"

"That dished you."

"By no means. I said in broken French that what I really was, was Armenian."

"Rash," said Jonathan. "I bet they had an Armenian waiter."

"Two. *And* the manager."

"So?"

"So I stammered that they'd misunderstood and what I *really* only spoke was Urdu."

"That fixed them, surely?"

"Yes and no. It fixed *them*. But as I was trying to think of the broken French for 'I speak only Urdu' a tweedy chap suddenly appeared and started speaking Urdu. I'd never heard it before. Rather an attractive language. It turned out he was called Jumbo Barraclough, and—— "

"Jumbo," said Jonathan, "how marvellous."

35

"He was marvellous. He's probably a member of this club. Apparently he'd left the army and he was selling English textiles to Americans. He was selling them at that moment to some people with cigars. Odd, I thought it. He showed me up completely. But I must say he more or less bailed me out— "

"Jumbo" I heard from behind my shoulder, "Jumbo Barraclough bailed that chap out in America." The two elderly men of the cloak-room were eating steak and kidney pie at the next table.

"Jumbo always had some damned queer friends— "

"Yes, but there are limits."

"Not nowadays, Puffy. Not nowadays."

Christopher choked over a mouthful of potato. Rolling his eyes desperately, he tried to regain enough gravity to swallow: and Jonathan, who had been waving at a waiter, turned back to find both of us giggling helplessly.

"Why are you creaking in that terrible schoolgirl way?"

Christopher's face became grave. "This country, Major, is not what it was." He pointed his fork at me portentously. "Not by a long chalk."

"Shh, Christopher, really— "

"Truth will out," he said darkly. "I can't keep quiet when I see the kind of thing we're coming to— "

"Boy's right," said the high, ripe voice behind me. "Bounder, I daresay, but he's right. Tell you what's wrong with this country, Puffy— "

"Did you go to the Metropolitan at all, Christopher?" said Jonathan, obviously realizing that our neighbours' conversation was dynamite.

"Yes, indeed. I saw—let's think— " he made a visible effort to behave.

"Too many damned niggers," came the penetrating old voice, "that's the trouble. Walking along St. James's Street this morning I saw half a dozen Fuzzy-Wuzzies in half a dozen minutes. You can't expect a country to survive that kind of damned infiltration—— "

"Yes?" said Jonathan desperately, "you saw—— ?"

"*Tosca*" gasped Christopher, "and—— "

"Ah, dear *Tosca*, I always think—— "

"And, kuk kuk—— "

"Christopher, *shh*—— "

"—kuk *Carmen*—— "

"Ah, *Carmen*, well I don't know that I—— "

"Tight, Puffy. Said he was a bounder. Who's that old bounder? And they've got that bounderish major—R.I.A.O.C. indeed—— "

"The chaps some chaps ask here—— "

"And *Bo-o-ohème*," gasped Christopher, purpling.

"Control yourself, Christopher—— " But it was no good. Jonathan himself was beginning to heave, his rigid facial control showing larger and larger cracks like a mudflat in earthquake country, and in a moment we were all laughing helplessly.

"Shall I write my complaint in the third person or the first person, Puffy? Rather fancy the third person myself—make it sound so damned nasty—— "

"No, do it so you can sign it. Then I'll sign it too."

"Ah, yes. Good idea. We might get some other signatures—— "

When we were collecting our hats and umbrellas from the cloak-room Christopher excused himself and hurried off. He came back five minutes later and joined us in the hall.

"Where have you been?"

"Talking to those old boys at the next table."

"Good God," said Jonathan. "What on earth did you say?"

"I apologized. I said I'd been abroad for five years and only just got back and hadn't seen you all that time and felt so high-spirited and all that, that I was afraid I may have behaved rather badly at lunch and would they please forgive me."

"How did that go down?"

"Like a dinner. They offered me a glass of brandy, actually—they wanted news of Jumbo, they said."

"But you didn't?"

"No. I said I never drank spirits at lunchtime. Which is true, as it happens."

"Good God. Well done."

"What *was* rather fun was, we composed their letter of complaint. 'Colonel Cracker-Jackson presents his compliments to the Committee, and begs to enquire when the dining-room was converted into a bear-garden—— '"

"Is his name really Colonel Cracker-Jackson?" I asked.

"Well, it ought to be. Actually it's Smith."

"What a shame."

"Yes, he rather feels that."

It wasn't a trick with Christopher. For him life *was* funnier and more vivid, and in his company one saw the world through spectacles half rose-tinted and half green: 3D spectacles. I once saw a film called *House of Wax* through such spectacles; Christopher's made everything into a house of cards: *Alice in Wonderland* cards. I miss him very much.

Chapter Three

✦

I had arranged to meet Sue that evening at a large pub near her flat. It had become unusual that we should see each other on consecutive days, and I was a little uneasy about it. She was so nice. We had shared so much enjoyment. I felt sentimental about our relationship and anxious that no hurt or hard feelings should come of its demise. She had rung me up at the office to make the date: I wondered if she saw the end as clearly as I did and less complaisantly. She knew very few people in London and did very little: I wondered if she were making me more central in her life that I had any mind to be—than was any good for either of us.

But it was nice drinking beer with her among the barley-sugar decorations of the saloon bar of the pub.

A florid man in a teddy-bear coat was sitting near us. A middle-aged blonde sat beside him; a pink gin sat in front of him.

"What's the French for *Skol*?" we heard him say, and we caught each other's eyes and laughed.

On our other side, a statuesque girl was drinking brown ale with a bearded man.

"I've decided to learn the guitar," she said; and again we laughed.

A rapid, slightly cockney voice came to us from behind,

growing in comprehensibility as its owner approached: "—never have a chance like this again, never," we heard. "Why are you *being* like this? I can't think why you're *being* like this."

"Perkins!" I said to Sue.

"Who?"

"You know—the spy."

"Last night's spy? The peak-party spy?"

"Yes. He's just behind us."

"Golly." She giggled and looked round. Perkins was talking to a big man in a duffle-coat, who looked bored. "—*tax-free*" he was saying, "don't you see the beauty of that? *Tax-free. . . .*"

"No, Perkins. Nothing doing."

"But *listen*, Sergei——"

"Oh shut up, for God's sake. Go away."

The big man walked to the bar and ordered a pint of bitter; Perkins was left, infinitely crestfallen, in the middle of a wide declamatory gesture. He held this pose for a ludicrously long time, his hands spread apart, his face mutely, pinkly appealing. Then he noticed me. He contracted like a quickly folding map, and his expression switched to a smile of eager greeting.

"Aha," he cried, "well met. Well met indeed."

"Good evening," I said.

He bowed to Sue, jauntily, from the hips. "And your good lady."

"Hullo," said Sue, her eyebrows raised in wonder.

"Mind if I join you?" he turned to the man in the teddy-bear coat. "Using this chair, sir? No? Right-ho, good, many thanks. Well." He sat stockily down. "Well well." Then he leapt to his feet again. "What's your poison? Ale? Two glasses of ale?"

"Er, thank you," said Sue.

He bustled away to the bar.

"That isn't a bit how I imagined him," said Sue. "You didn't make him sound a bit like that."

"He wasn't like this last night," I said.

"He's rather nice like this."

"It's certainly better," I agreed.

"Bitter?" said Perkins, returning. "Just what I've got you. All right? Good. Splendid. Well." With elaborate care he put three pint tankards down on the table, sat down himself, and buried his round face in the froth. "Ale," he said, "nothing like it, nothing. Now you're just the people I wanted to see. Providential, running into you like this."

"Do you want some more copy for your book?" asked Sue.

"Ah no, dear lady," he waved a hand graciously. "Your good man and I discussed the matter yesterday evening— he may have mentioned it to you—and I have consented to suspend my observations in deference to—— "

"Well *really*—— " I began.

"Not a word," said Perkins, "not a word. I don't blame you in the least. I daresay, if I were so placed myself, I should take just the same line—well, at least, if I knew that a work of art *depended*—but there, I mustn't let my hobby-horse run away with me—I mustn't bore you with my shop—I mustn't. . . ."

"No," I said.

"Well," said Perkins. "To business."

"Business?" said Sue and I together.

"Business," he repeated. "Distasteful word, but in this case I fancy it combines with pleasure—a kind of relaxation, anyway, and by no means without interest to an observer of human—there! Away goes my tongue again." He turned to me. "You, sir, are my child."

"What?"

"My child. I spoke to Maggie and Ferd today, and

41

Frankie—I went round and saw them all—and they've agreed that you can be enrolled as of yesterday, although *technically*, since you didn't pay your half-crown, you shouldn't be enrolled until today. But we're all prepared to waive that irregularity in the interests of the whole mountain."

"Ah," I said, "I'm with you."

"Now you *should* be taking your children to Billie's tonight—— "

"I can't possibly—— "

"Quite, my dear fellow, quite. We understand, I assure you. We don't expect the impossible. As it happens, my other child is placed the same way. It's all very unfortunate, but we realize it can't be helped. You'll be interested to meet your sister, by the by, ha ha—— "

"Ha ha."

"—a most challenging mind. Well. So what we've arranged is that you, and your two children, and *their* children, shall *all* come to *my* peak-party tomorrow evening. I do hope," he looked at me severely, "I do hope we can rely on you. It's most important there should be no shilly-shallying—— "

"No, no, quite," I said. "Can we go to Mr. Perkins's peak-party tomorrow night, Sue?"

"Yes," said Sue. "Thank you, Mr. Perkins."

Perkins blushed. "Call me Perkins," he said. "All my friends do."

"Hm," said Sue. "We've got to get a lot of other people."

"Yes," I said. "I'll have to get another child, and you and the other child will both have to get two people—and we've all got to be free tomorrow evening."

"Mm. . . ."

"I'll get someone at the office, perhaps—— "

"I expect we'll manage."

"I do hope so," said Perkins earnestly. "I can't exaggerate

the importance to all of us. . . . A few backsliders, and the whole Everest is threatened. A few incompetents, and—— "

"Yes," I said, "yes."

"Well," said Perkins rising, "if you'll excuse me—I've got to go and see Billie again, and I thought I'd better look in on Frankie—— "

"Yes—— "

"Till tomorrow night, then! You know your way, I think —yes, to be sure you do—— "

"Yes. Yes, I do."

"Splendid, splendid. About nine."

"Right."

"Thank you for the beer," said Sue.

"A pleasure. Nothing but a pleasure. Well. *Adios!*"

"*Adios*" I said faintly.

When his wide back had disappeared I turned to Sue. "I *suppose* we're in this thing?"

She smiled and shrugged. "I suppose we are."

The trouble was, sponsorship by Perkins removed the whole project from the realm of the likely—even the attractive—into the inconceivable. Last night, and put as our copy of the rules put it, the idea had seemed perfectly feasible. This evening, put as Perkins put it, it seemed a pipe-dream— a mirage all of a piece with his hopeful, hopeless, enormous book.

"He's rather sweet," said Sue. "He's trusting us. We mustn't let him down."

"*Sweet*—— "

"Well, you couldn't be expected to see that, really, could you? Not after last night."

"I should have thought *you*, after last night—— "

"Oh well. People are so odd—— "

Thus half-heartedly we decided we were enrolled in the Everest Club.

A little after half-past ten the next morning Christopher came exuberantly into my office. He was elegantly tweeded, and wearing a flame-coloured rose-bud in his buttonhole.

"Good God," I said, "are you on strength already?"

"Ensign Townsend reporting, sir." He came stiffly but crookedly to attention, and most of his body performed a fanciful salute.

"Carry on, please," I said. "Quick posting."

He subsided on to the edge of my desk. "Oh well, I don't believe in shilly-shallying."

This reminded me of Perkins. "Oh, by the way," I said, "will you be my child?"

"Of course," he cried, "of course. What can you mean?"

I explained about the Everest Club. "It's too absurd," I finished, "but we seem to have let ourselves in for it. I wondered if it would amuse you at all to—— "

"*Amuse* me?" He seemed delighted. "Nonsense. This is a magnificent idea. Exactly suited to my administrative talents. You may rely on me completely. Certainly I shall be your child. I shall take it extremely seriously—in fact I shall begin taking it extremely seriously now. Let's see—I've got to get two children by tonight, haven't I, hm—— "

"You're free tonight?"

"I shall *make* myself free. Well, actually I am free. I wonder what Uncle Jonathan's doing this evening. . . ?"

"*Jonathan?*"

"An excellent candidate. Very serious. Reliable. You'll allow that, Major? Reliable?"

"Oh, well, yes—— "

"And that secretary of his, what about her? Laburnum or something."

"Lavinia. But, really, do you think—— "

"Why not? Lots of friends, I imagine?"

"Yes, certainly, but—— "

44

"Quite a qualification, I should have thought."

I considered this. "Yes. That's perfectly true. But, Christopher, *picture* her friends. . . ."

"Gay as larks, I expect. Besides," he went on stiffly, "leave my grandchildren out of this."

"My great-grandchildren."

"Don't start coming the stuffy parent, for God's sake. This is the twentieth century, father, things are different—— "

"Damned unfilial, your attitude. Young puppy—— "

"Oh I didn't mean it, daddy, honestly—— "

At this moment Jacqueline's startled head, dressed as to the hair in a new and grotesque style, peered round the door.

"Er, Mr. Melot—— "

"Yes, Jacqueline?"

"Did you call me?"

"No. Er, no."

She came the rest of the way into the room. "Oh, I thought you did." She looked at me wistfully. Knowing what was coming I clenched my knuckles.

It came. "You haven't said how you like my new hair-style."

"I like it very much, Jacqueline, *very* much—it suits you awfully well—— "

"Let's have a proper look," said Christopher. "Hair-styles are very important. Come over to the light—*that's* better. . . . Would you like my frank opinion?"

"Oh. . . ."

"Christopher. . . ." I said warningly.

"With you in a moment, Major. At present I am giving this young lady's hair-style my full attention. No less than it deserves. Hm," he considered it through half-closed eyes, "hm. I think—and I'm speaking as something of an expert— I *think* it ought to be a shade more off the face. I think the

45

hair should frame the brow, instead of covering it up. Here, look at this mirror. See what I mean? More up *here*—— " he gestured with his hands about his own brow.

He was right, of course. The *ingénue* fringe Jacqueline had adopted looked terrible above her high, spinsterish nose. But he shouldn't be saying so. Jacqueline would have a fit.

"Christopher . . ." I warned again.

"Oh," said Jacqueline. She was staring unfathomably at her mud-coloured reflection, prodding experimentally at her lack-lustre curls. "Oh." Suddenly she turned, radiant. "Do you know, Mr. Townsend, I believe you're right? Thank you ever so much. I'll try it this evening. Or in the lunch-hour, perhaps, I might try it. . . ."

"*Do.*"

"Well. Thanks *so* much again. Sure there was nothing, Mr. Melot?"

"No, nothing, thank you, Jacqueline."

She nodded, beaming, and left.

"Christopher, really—— "

"Made her day."

"That's true, but—— "

"Well then?"

"Oh nothing."

At four o'clock Sue rang up.

"Everest," she announced.

"Ah yes. How's it going?"

"Well, rather oddly. I got one person—Godfrey Peters, I think you've met him?—— "

"Chap with a moustache?"

"That's right. Well, I tried and *tried*—— "

"Oh Sue—— "

"Yes, well, but it ended all right. I ran into Perkins again—— "

"Good God."

"Darling, you must stop saying 'Good God' like that. It makes you sound about eighty-seven."

"Oh—all right. Well?"

"Well, Perkins. He said had I got my two, and I said no, only one, and he said *good* because his sister wants to join, and—— "

"So she's your other child?"

"Yes, isn't it lucky?"

"What can she be like?"

"I daren't think. We'll know this evening, anyway. Who have you got?"

"Well, Christopher Townsend, a man I used to—— "

"I know. You never stopped talking about him last night."

"Oh—sorry. Was I a bore?"

"Not a bit. He sounds fascinating. I'm dying to meet him."

I replied jokingly, automatically: "Oy oy."

"Oh darling," she said quickly, "you know it's you I love."

"Oh good," I said unhappily.

"Who are his children?"

"Christopher's? He's got Jonathan Cornish, our boss—— "

"Golly."

"Yes. And Jonathan's secretary. Girl called Lavinia Laud.'

"The Hon. Lavinia Laud—oh dear, I've heard about her. She'll terrify me."

"She terrifies me."

"Oh dear. Where are we meeting?"

"The pub at nine. But I'll give you dinner first, shall I?"

"No, I'll give you dinner here."

"Oh darling, are you sure? That makes three nights running. . . . Well, lovely. About seven-thirty?"

"Any time. Earlier the better."

"Right—— "

We said good-bye and I hung up. Oh dear, I thought, oh dear oh dear. This is going to get more and more difficult the longer I leave it. If only she weren't so *nice*——

I spent a large part of the afternoon on the telephone. At a quarter to three a friend of mine in the Ministry of Health rang up to lay, as he said, a proposition before me.

"What sort of proposition?" I asked.

"It's a little difficult to explain," he said in his strong, over-modulated, committee-room voice, "but basically the idea is a streamlined version of the old chain-letter system—you know the business I mean—— "

"Ah," I said, "you're talking about—— "

"It's a very ingenious idea." He sailed as serenely over my interruption as a line over a piece of driftwood. "I'll try to put in terms that you'll understand—— "

"Don't bother," I said.

"What? You haven't even heard about it yet. You really mustn't prejudge this issue, Eddie, because I assure you— I've looked into it quite closely—— "

"No no," I said, "you don't understand. I'm in it—— "

"—really quite closely, and the idea's absolutely valid provided enough sensible people—— "

"—*in it already*," I shouted.

"In the Everest Club?"

"Yes." .

"Ah. Ah, yes, I see. In that case there's no particular point in my—— "

"No."

"No. Well, anyway, we must have lunch together one of these days, Eddie."

"Yes, we must."

"I'll ring you up, shall I? Or will *you* ring *me* up?"

48

"You ring me up."

"All right."

At half-past three another friend rang up—a man who wrote articles for magazines. His articles had names like *Glyndebourne—Musical Mecca in the Heart of Sussex* and *A Cockney Heritage—Is Rhyming Slang Dying Out?* He was always thinking of starting magazines, and would from time to time get in touch with me to interest me in some phantasmagorial periodical: so I was expecting him to begin: "*Eddie*, I have a wonderful new project—you must come in on it—a fortnightly dealing with Social Life and the Electrical Trade—it's an entirely new combination, bound to catch on—I thought of calling it *Spark*—— "

Instead he began: "*Eddie*, there's a wonderful new project—a thing called the Everest Club—you must join, it's going to be a gold-mine, really a winner—— "

"I'm already in."

"Oh. Well, in that case, come in *again*—no reason why not—double your money—— "

"Well, no, I don't think I will actually thanks awfully—— "

"No? Perhaps you're right. Well, we *must* have lunch together one of these days, anyway—what about next Tuesday? As a matter of fact there's something I particularly want to talk to you about—a new idea I've had—— "

"I can't do Tuesday, I'm afraid."

"Oh, pity, well, never mind. I'll ring you up shall I?"

"Yes, or I might ring you up—— "

At a quarter-past four a girl who worked on a fashion magazine rang me up.

"Eddie, it's dreadfully short notice, I'm afraid, but wonder if you can come for a drink tomorrow evening?"

"I'd love to, but the thing is, what time? Because—— "

49

"After dinner."

"Well, alas I can't, then—— "

"Come in just for a minute, I mean *literally* only ten minutes if you're in a hurry—actually it's not just a party, it's a new club thing, we're all going to make hundreds of pounds—— "

"Oh, well, I'm already in. it, I'm afraid."

"*Oh* how annoying. I was sure you wouldn't be."

"What *do* you mean by that?"

"Well," she said, "it's really a compliment, in a way—— "

"Oh, ha ha, good. Anyway we must have lunch together —shall I ring you up one of these days?"

"Yes *do*."

At ten to five another girl rang up—the bored young wife of a friend of mine.

"I bet I know what you're going to say," I said.

"I bet you don't."

"How much?"

"Ten bob."

"Right. What are you going to say?"

"*Oh* no—that's too easy. If I say first then you can always pretend afterwards that whatever I say is what you thought I was going to say. *You* say why *you* think I'm ringing up, and then I'll tell you if you're right."

"No—that's too easy for *you*. If I say first, then you can pretend—oh, the hell with it. Everest."

"*Everest*. I've been trying to remember all day what the dam' thing was called. Oh dear. That *is* what I'm ringing up about."

"I'm in it already."

"Oh *dear*. You were practically my last hope."

"Thank you."

"Well, you know what I mean. Do I owe you ten shillings?"

"Yes, certainly."

"Oh dear. Well, you must come to dinner, Eddie, or—or a drink or something, anyway soon—— "

"I'd love to."

"Good. I'll ring you up, then, shall I?"

As I opened my evening paper on the bus that evening, two very ugly girls sat down in front of me.

"It's getting hopeless," said one. "Utterly hopeless."

"Everyone's in it," agreed the other sombrely. "What are we to do?"

"I even asked Mr. Bonebridge this afternoon—that's how desperate I'm getting."

"Mr. *Bonebridge*? Ooh, will he come in?"

"No. Doesn't approve of it, he says, been caught before—— "

"Ooh. Well, if you're my only child and Reg is *your* only child—— "

"We won't have much of a mountain."

"No. Seems a shame, really, all that money—— "

Sue gave me spaghetti and some rather horrible red wine, and then we went to the pub to meet the rest of our mountain. We were the first to get there, so we sat drinking beer and listening to the pretentious conversations round us.

Presently Godfrey Peters appeared. Sue's child was a stocky, dark-complexioned man doing very well in (I think) the wholesale shoe business. As Sue from time to time rebukingly told me, he was very kind. He talked incessantly, always about his friends. These friends were unknown to me, though Sue had met some of them. Some were journalists who knew the Soho and Notting Hill crime belts intimately and who were the recipients of all kinds of surprising confidences from elder statesmen and senior officials.

Some were actors whose meteoric careers were being systematically thwarted by more eminent players, all of whom
were motivated either by jealousy, or, obscurely, by various
forms of esoteric sexual perversion. None, as far as I know,
were in the wholesale shoe business. (Sue, of course, fell
into the thwarted-actor class: Sue, whose attitude to the
stage consisted of surprise that she was on it at all, together with almost complete refusal to do anything about
being on it, together with the well-founded suspicion that
she was a terrible actress. I used to wonder how Godfrey
rated me until a colleague, one morning, told me he had
heard a French-looking man in a Hampstead pub quoting
with awe my views on the future of sterling convertability.)

"—the Tiger's got about thirty tearaways now," he was
telling Sue as I came back from getting him a drink at the
bar. "They know he did the Granada job *and* the Pembridge
Gardens job, but they can't lay a finger on him. Protection.
Dick was telling me about it at Pat's party last night—— "

"Dick?"

"Dick's the bloke I know on the Ban—great friend of
mine—— "

"On the what?"

"The *Daily Banner*. He knows all those Clapham boys.
He says the whole Clapham lot are getting organized now
under Shiner Kelly—you know, the boy who used to work
for Jack Olivetti on the race-tracks before the war. Dick
knows all about it. Why, Jack himself came up to him once,
in the French pub, and said—— "

A cry of "Major" behind us interrupted this puzzling
narrative, and we were joined by Jonathan, Christopher and
Lavinia. I performed introductions, and Jonathan went over
to the bar with Lavinia to get some more drinks.

"So *you're* Sue," said Christopher, "—(I may call you Sue?)
—the Major told me about you, but being a pedestrian old

body like so many of these regular soldiers—can't express himself with the exactness one would wish in a leader of men—he described you most inadequately—— "

"Oh. . . . He described you *quite* adequately, I should say."

"As to appearance, you mean? He mentioned my Grecian profile? He enlarged upon the way my hair curls over the ears?"

"That, yes. But as to manner, I meant, more."

"Ah, *manner*. Well—— "

Godfrey leaned over to me. "Lavinia *Laud*, did you say?"

"Yes."

"Ah yes. Middlewick's girl, of course. Rupert's sister."

I was surprised. "Do you know Rupert?"

"Well, I don't suppose he'd remember me—— "

"What's our E.T.A., Major?" asked Christopher.

"E.T.A. twenty-one hundred hours local time."

"Then we ought to cross the start-line fairly soon."

"Not just yet," said Jonathan returning. "Not after I've bought all these blasted glasses of beer. Sure you can manage Lavinia? O good—— "

"What's the French for *Skol*?" I said to Sue.

"I don't know," she said, "all I can tell you is that I've decided to learn the guitar."

"*Have* you?" said Godfrey. "Do you know, so have I. Richard was telling me only the other day that he knows a brilliant teacher, absolutely brilliant, who had to leave Spain because Segovia—— "

"Richard? Same as Dick?"

"No, *no*, quite different. Anyway, this man, this teacher—— "

"I've just started learning it too," said Lavinia.

Sue giggled, then squeaked when I kicked her ankle.

"*Are* you?" said Godfrey. "Have you got a good teacher?"

53

"Very good indeed. English, actually, but a lot of people think she's the best—several of us go to her—— "

"May one ask her name?" (I could hear him, in a day or two, saying: "Lavinia was telling me just the other night—yes, Lavinia Laud—well, I wouldn't call her a *great friend*, exactly—— ").

"Time your company was leaving the Assembly Area, Major."

"Yes," I agreed. "Are we all ready?"

As we walked the short distance to the house where, only two nights before, I had met Perkins, Christopher fell in beside me.

"That's a very good girl."

"Sue?"

"Yes. Very good indeed."

"I think so too. I like her very much."

"And lovely."

"And lovely, yes."

"You're a lucky old thing, Major."

"Yes," I said heavily, "yes."

Perkins's small sitting-room was already crowded when we arrived.

"What ho!" cried Perkins, "what ho, what ho. Come along in. What's your poison, sir? We'll do the introductions and things later, shall we?—first things first, I always say—business before pleasure—— "

"Er, have you any beer?" said Jonathan.

"*Beer*. . . . Well, is cider any good?"

"Cider's fine," said Jonathan faintly.

We all had cider, since it was all there was, in an extravagantly varied collection of glasses. I had a dark red, long-stemmed wine-glass of the kind from which undergraduates drink Chianti; Jonathan had a tooth-mug; Lavinia,

I was glad to see, had the plastic top of a thermos. When we were all equipped with these vessels I introduced my side of the mountain, and Perkins presented the other side. "Miss Bloom, my other child," he said; "Miss Bloom's children, Mr. and Mrs. Klondyke; *their* children. . . ." Then he said, bowing to Sue, "and this is *your* other child, madame, my sister Clare."

"Oh good," said Sue, "how do you do? This is your brother, Godfrey Peters—— "

"Pleased to meet you."

Miss Perkins was a surprise. I don't know quite what I'd expected—I hadn't thought about it much, but in so far as I expected anything I suppose it was a female Perkins, plump and pink, that I looked to see. In fact she was small, slim, rather brassily fair, with a sharp, pretty little face. She looked about twenty-eight. Everything about her said "secretary"; everything about her said "bitch".

I found myself beside Miss Bloom.

"Well," I said heartily, "so we're brother and sister."

"Yes," she simpered, barely audibly.

"Had any trouble getting children?"

"No."

"Ah, good, got them easily eh? Well. I gather some people have been having a lot of trouble."

"Have they?" she whispered.

"Yes indeed. Why, several people rang me up only this afternoon, wanting me to join. I had to say no, I was in it already. One or two of them told me they were finding it *very* difficult, getting hold of people."

"Oh."

"Well! What about another glass of cider? Oh—there isn't any. Well—— "

Lavinia and Godfrey were discussing the guitar.

"Half the Flamenco players in Spain today aren't gipsies at all," he was saying. "They're Algerians and Portuguese cashing in on the tourist trade."

"Really? How on earth do you know all this?"

"David was telling me. Do you know David? David Stubbs? Brilliant actor, really brilliant, great friend of mine. Poor David—he's had shocking luck. He was offered some wonderful parts last year, but Douglas stepped in every time and kiboshed it—pure jealousy—— "

"Douglas?"

"Old Douglas Foxley."

"Really? Do you know him?"

"Well, I don't suppose he'd remember me—— "

"He's a wonderful actor, don't you think?"

"Wonderful? Well, in a very limited way, I suppose, yes, a very narrow range, and as Joe was saying the other day, Douglas's personal habits have to be obscene to be believed, ha ha."

"Oh, how marvellous, but do tell me, what *are* his personal habits?"

"Well, for *one* thing—— "

Christopher was talking to the Klondykes.

"Puppets aren't what they were," piped Mr. Klondyke, "not by any manner of means. All these Russians, now, and Czechs coming over, not the thing at all, I assure you."

"Is the technique different?" asked Christopher with grave interest.

"No no, not the technique so much—in fact in their way they're very adequate technicians—it's more the aesthetic that's wrong—— "

"A certain crudity? A certain obviousness?"

"That's it! I can see you appreciate what we old school of puppet-masters call—— "

"Don't let Jerome run *on*, Mr. er," boomed Mrs. Klon-dyke, "he does run on if you give him half a chance, ha ha, of course we both feel it deeply—all true puppeteers must—— "

"Of course," said Christopher, "to any artist, seeing the standards of his medium debased—— "

"Exactly! What we always say—— "

Over by the window Jonathan was talking to Clare.

"—no, as a matter of fact I'm an advertising agent."

"Oh, that must be frightfully interesting."

"Yes, it is, very."

"You must meet so many interesting people."

"Yes, I do indeed."

"I'm sure you have to be very clever."

"*I* don't have to be, luckily. I just employ clever people."

"Now I don't believe that, not for a moment—— "

At this point Perkins started talking to me about the Everest Club, so I missed the rest. Poor Jonathan, I thought. He was having as bad a time as I'd had with Miss Bloom, only in a different and even worse way.

Presently Perkins stood on his small green armchair and clapped his hands for silence.

"To business," he cried, "to business. It is my duty and privilege to expound to you, as my descendants, the idea and procedure of the Everest Club, to which we welcome you this evening—— "

"I like your Mr. Townsend," Sue told me an hour and a half later.

"Good. I'm glad you do. He likes you, too."

"Oh, good."

"What did you think of Jonathan?"

"Heaven. Absolute heaven."

"Yes, he takes all the girls that way."

"I don't wonder. Lavinia's rather a pill, I must say."

"A number nine," I agreed, "a regular Carter."

"The Klondykes were quite sweet."

"The puppeteers? Yes, I liked them. What did you make of Perkins's sister?"

"Hard to say. Intelligent."

"Oh? A bitch, I thought."

"Could be. Very pretty."

"Ye-es, if you like that kind of thing."

"Plenty of people do."

"Oh yes, plenty of people do."

Another hour later I was alone. I was feeling irritated and depressed, and puzzled that I should feel irritated and depressed. What was this burr in my hair, this thorn in my soft pink side? Driving home I searched for it, and found it finally in Sue's remarks after the end of the party. "I like Christopher Townsend," she had said. "Jonathan is heaven, absolute heaven."

Jealous. I was jealous.

Chapter Four

✣

A t half-past eleven the following morning (it was Thursday) Jonathan asked me to go and see him.

Passing Jacqueline I said: "I'm just off to see the Chairman. I don't suppose I shall be long."

"Very well, Mr. Melot. Er," she paused.

"I like your hair *very* much the way you've got it now," I lied, "it's a great improvement."

"Oh thank you, Mr. Melot, thanks ever so much. Wasn't it clever of Mr. Townsend?"

"Yes, very clever."

Passing Lavinia I said: "I hope you enjoyed the peak-party."

"Wasn't it amusing?" she said. "What a *galère*. Some very interesting people there, though, I mean, one or two—— "

"Oh, very."

Jonathan said: "Morning, Eddie. How nice of you to come. Look, I wonder if you can help me out of a jam?"

"Well, of course, Jonathan—— "

"Well, I'm supposed to be lunching with a man called Robinson. He's from the North. I hope he's going to be a client. The idea was that I should tell him all about the agency—you, know, the usual stuff, and I now find I can't do it. I've made some kind of nonsense with the dates—— "

"Shall I pinch-hit?"

"Is it frightfully inconvenient?"

"Not a bit."

"It would be awfully kind, Eddie. I'd better tell you about Mr. Robinson—— "

He did, and presently I was sitting in the bar at the Connaught ordering a dry Martini for Mr. Robinson. He was a big, whitish man who made zip-fasteners in Halifax; he did become a client; he was very nice.

I quite enjoyed lunch, and I thought no more about the substitution of myself for Jonathan. Why should I? But it was the first inkling any of us might have had.

My flat (conveniently situated in an agreeable slum behind Victoria Street) was to be the scene , that evening, of my peak-party. My Everest Club grandchildren, four of them, were supposed to be bringing two recruits each to pay their half-crowns and join in the fun. So I dined early in a small nearby restaurant; at nine o'clock I was making coffee in a large jug; at nine forty-five Lavinia arrived with two girls.

"This is Eddie Melot, one of my colleagues," she said. "Victoria Crabbe, Angelica Blacker-Boatman."

"How do you do?"

"Ah good," cried Miss Blacker-Boatman (plump and dark) noticing a Henry Moore reproduction hanging in my narrow hall, "ah good. I've got this in my loo." She turned to Lavinia: "I?" or it may have been "Ay?"

"Well," said Lavinia. dubiously, "yes, on the whole."

"Ah—— "

I could make nothing of this, so I led the way into the sitting-room and said: "Have some coffee."

"Look," cried Lady Victoria (thin and reddish) picking up a recent picaresque novel by a young female don, "look. Sara's." She turned to Lavinia: "I., surely."

"Yes—— "

"G.?" or it may have been "Gee?"

"Well, near enough."

"Ah——"

Baffled, I said: "Black or white?"

"Black, of *course*"

"I didn't realize you were in the same firm as Lavinia," said Victoria accusingly.

"He's quite important," said Lavinia as though it were a joke. Well, it was, rather.

"Oh—what do you do?"

"Marketing," I said, "and research and things."

"How very peculiar."

"Why?"

"Oh well—Did you choose this wallpaper?"

"No, it was here when I came."

"Oh I *see*. It's charming."

"It's quite pretty," I said, "yes." It was a very ordinary greenish stripe: quite pretty.

"It's charming," repeated Victoria.

"Are these all your books?" said Angelica, peering.

"Yes."

"Mm. Gide, yes, Melville, Proust—ah yes. And *The Specialist*—I love *The Specialist*."

"I used to," said Lavinia.

"Yes," said Victoria. "It's a bit F., you know, Angie."

"F.?" I asked.

"Freshman," they explained.

"Well, perhaps," said Angelica, considering. "Yes. Chandler, Powell," she turned back to the parti-coloured shelves, "O'Hara, Salinger, yes, Waugh, Ian Fleming—You don't seem to have any Graham Greene?"

"No," I agreed.

"Or Ivy C.-B.?"

"No."

61

"Pity."

"Oh, I don't know—— "

"No," she looked at me with contempt. Then she said to Lavinia: "Mm, I., but—— "

"Yes," agreed Lavinia. "H., though."

"Oh well, that's something."

"What *are* you talking about?" I said.

"You."

"Yes I know, but what are you saying?"

"Ha ha," they said, "wouldn't you like to know?"

"Very much," I lied, "very much."

"Ha ha."

This depressing business was interrupted by Jonathan and two companions.

"My children, Eddie," he said, "is that the word, children? This game of yours is the damnedest thing. George you know, of course, and Mr. Robinson tells me you gave him a very good lunch—— "

"Oh, good evening Mr. Robinson, very nice to see you here—hullo George—do you know what you're letting yourselves in for?"

"Eh, well, Mr. Cornish did say you were goin' to make us all rich—— "

"That's right, ha ha—— "

Godfrey Peters arrived almost immediately, also, I was glad to see, with two companions.

" —David Stubbs, and this is Dick—— "

"Of the Ban?"

"Oh, you've met my small efforts, very gratifying, ha ha—— "

"Yes indeed, who hasn't?"

"Hul*lo*," said Lavinia, "now, Godfrey Peters, Victoria Crabbe, Angelica Blacker-Boatman—— "

"How do you do?"

"I.," she murmured loudly.

"Oh *good*, how do you do?"

"David Stubbs, Lavinia Laud—— "

"*The* David Stubbs?"

"Is there one?"

"Oh, ha ha, how marvellous—well of *course*—— "

"And this is Dick."

"Dick?"

"Of the Ban."

"The what?"

Sue and Christopher arrived together. Neither was bound to come by the rules of the Everest Club, since their children and not they were responsible for the new generation of half-crown-paying recruits. But I had, of course, expected them. What I hadn't expected was that they would arrive together, having dined together: and I didn't like it.

"Hullo," said Lavinia coldly, "oh hul*lo* Christopher."

"Sue, how nice to see you," said Jonathan. "May I intro-duce Mr. Robinson—I hope a client, if Eddie did his job—?"

"Eh, certainly a client."

"Oh *good*—I say, Eddie you've got us some new business we're very glad indeed to have—— "

"You don't mind my giving Sue dinner, Major?"

"No of course not, Christopher—— "

"I mean, don't, because—— "

"No."

"Christopher," said Lavinia, "come and meet Les Girls."

"Er, delighted. But I know you, don't I—Angelica Volga-Boatman?"

"Ha ha, *Blacker*-Boatman—— "

"Have some more coffee?" I said, "and how's your glass —ah, we must do something about that, er, red or white, was it?"

63

"I hope," said Sue, "Mr. Cornish knows what he's doing, letting you in for this crazy affair, Mr. Robinson?"

"Well, I'm not staying South, so I'm not really goin' to be able, more's the pity, I *will* say, seems like great fun—— "

"Oh, yes, it is a pity—— "

"The production was devastating," shrilled David, "and they wanted me to wear garments such as you've never seen the like of, so I said quite firmly—— "

"Wasn't that the time Douglas—— ?"

"Don't *talk* about it, Godfrey—— "

"Douglas?"

"Old Doug Foxley."

"Oh *really*? Now tell me—— "

"A hell of a party, Major," murmured Christopher.

"What a bunch," I agreed. "Look at those damned blue-stocking smarties—— "

"Oh, those little girls? Poor little things."

"They're eating the honest Peters."

"And he's eating them, which is very nice and fortunate all round."

"There's that, certainly—— "

"Eh, Mr. Melot, must break it to you, shan't be able to stay in this business, I'm afraid, I'm really sorry—— "

"Oh, what a pity, you've got to go back North of course—— "

"Lord love a duck, Eddie," said George, a commercial artist and a colleague of Jonathan's and mine, "Lord slap me with a fish, what a crew you have collected. Where did you find the nancy?"

"He's a brilliant actor," I said. "Don't be rude about my guests."

George made a small, obscene gesture, and began to search, with ill-simulated absent-mindedness, for the sort of cupboard the whisky might be kept in.

64

"There isn't any," I said.

"Bloody hell fire, I come all the way to bloody Pim-lico—— "

"Westminster."

"Practically *Lambeth*, and there's no bloody drink."

"Have some wine?"

"*Wine*? You know me Eddie, you know my teeny weak-nesses—don't tease an old man—— "

The bell rang again, and Clare appeared.

"Not G. or I.," I heard Lavinia murmur.

"Shut up, Lavinia," I said.

"Not very H., you friend," said Victoria.

"Colleague," corrected Lavinia.

"H.?" I said incautiously.

"Ha ha, wouldn't you like to know?"

"Oh Mr. Cornish," said Clare, "I hoped you'd be here."

"Very nice to see you, too—— "

Poor Jonathan, I thought, caught again.

"What on earth?" said Angelica.

"You may well ask."

"Hm."

"Hullo, Clare," said Sue, "brought any children?"

"Er, hullo, no, I'm afraid not—but Mr. Cornish," she turned back to the animated conversation she had just be-gun with Jonathan, "but Mr. Cornish, what do you do when you know a client's doing the wrong thing, but if you tell him so he gets so annoyed he goes off to someone else, not so good?"

"Well, that's one of our nightmares, of course, it's very difficult—— "

She was clever, then: fluttering her eyelashes *and* asking sensible questions. Poor Jonathan.

"Have a glass of wine, Mr. Robinson—you don't mind, do you Eddie—red? Fine, here we are—— "

"Bloody prawns in aspic, Eddie, have a heart—I've spotted a corkscrew and where there's a corkscrew——"

"There's a bottle of wine," I said. "The flesh is willing, George, but there just isn't any spirit."

"*Joke*, make bloody crumby *jokes*, when I'm feeling——"

"What a laughable lamp," said Victoria, "I mean, what a really lamentable lamp——"

"Oh well, you know, one does so agree, but——" the odious Stubbs waved his large white hands at my shabby, comfortable sofa.

"—such a pleasure to meet someone who's really I.——"

"I.?" said Godfrey.

"Intellectual," explained Lavinia. "We have to talk in initials because really some of the people one finds oneself with——"

"My dear, don't I know it, and as Joe was saying——"

"Yes, I see that, Mr. Cornish, I really do see that, but surely—I expect you'll think this is just silly—but surely the question of *who* you're selling to is answered by what you're selling?"

"Exactly," said Jonathan, "exactly right, very far from silly, and I only wish some of my executives saw that as clearly as you do——"

"Oh no——"

"—because of course, in a sense, a product defines its own market by its own characteristics—price, for instance."

"And I suppose the market kind of asks for things too? I mean, tells you what to make in the first place?"

Oh yes, I thought, clever, too clever by half, that little bit. Poor Jonathan, what a time he must be having, being systematically canvassed for a job.

"H. means humble," Lavinia was explaining, low-voiced.

"Ah——"

"And G. means—well," she checked herself hurriedly, "that's not one of the important ones—I. is what matters."

"Oh quite." Godfrey looked at her admiringly. "I must say. . . ." He dropped his voice. She smiled, with what they used to call a conscious look.

"Lovely," said Christopher, "see that? Touching."

"Isn't it bloody killing?"

"Don't be satirical, Major. It ill becomes you. Be glad."

"Oh, as to *glad*—— "

"And listen, please believe me about this dinner business—— "

"Oh yes," I said, "yes."

A little later I saw him laughing quietly with Sue in a corner and I felt sick and astounded and poured wine into glasses with an automatic, slighty shaking hand.

We did the Everest Club business soon after this: I explained the form and collected half-crowns. A certain retrenchment was necessary, since Robinson was a non-starter and Clare had brought no children: this was worked out satisfactorily and the charts were filled in accordingly. The I. girls thought this was all very amusing but not, I felt, quite G.

"Good-bye," they were saying presently, "thank you very much. *Good*-bye, Christopher. Well, Godfrey, if you're *really* going that way—— "

"—well, all right," Sue was saying, "thank you. But, Christopher, I don't know if Eddie—— "

"Don't mind me," I said, "for God's sake."

"Oh Eddie, this isn't a bit like you, how can you be so—— "

" 'Night, Eddie, many thanks."

"Oh, Jonathan, are you off? Good night, good night Mr, Robinson. . . . No, don't mind me—— "

"Eddie, *please*"

"You know me, Major," said Christopher soberly, "you *know* me."

"Yes, Christopher. Sorry. Being childish, I'm afraid—— "

"Well," said Sue, "yes."

"I'm sorry, Sue."

"Don't be. I'm pleased, in a way—— "

"Oh I see, yes," I said uncontrollably, horrified with myself, "that's it of course—— "

"Eddie—— "

"Sorry," I said wretchedly, "sorry."

Then they had all gone, and I uncovered the whisky-bottle and found a large, cleanish glass.

"Dear Eddie, I knew you wouldn't fail me in the end—— "

"Christ, are you still here?"

"A silly question, you know that, in the circumstances," said George, "and stinking rude, come to think of it. But never mind, *never* mind—— "

We drank the bottle between us. I slept quite well.

The next day I began to be busy. Not, I mean, that I had been notably idle for the past few weeks; but on that Friday I began to have one of those unpredictable, apparently causeless spells of desperate overwork that do happen, from time to time, in my ridiculous trade. The field-work results of no less than three different market surveys came in together, placed symmetrically on my desk by a gravely sympathetic Jacqueline; there was a heavy backlog of Belgravia Bond stuff to work out; Mr. Robinson's zip-fasteners required immediate and serious attention from my department; there were, as always in these spasms of crisis, many more horrid, fiddling little jobs even than usual.

None of this is in the least relevant to the story I am telling; but my being busy is one of the three things which, when I look back on that time, characterize those weeks for me. I started early in the morning. I hoped, day after day, to get time for lunch, and sent Jacqueline out, day after day, for sandwiches and bottled beer to eat in the office. I left at seven-thirty, eight, nine in the evenings. The evenings—well, the evenings. They were another feature of that odd time, as it will presently be the moment to explain. And the third thing: as to the third thing, that was strange, a very strange business.

That Friday was the day for Christopher and Sue to hold their respective peak-parties and collect their quota of half-crowns for the new Everest. Christopher told me, during a lull in the early afternoon, that they were holding a joint party. He asked me to come. I said I would. Sue rang up a little later with the same news and the same invitation. I said yes, again. But I didn't go. When nine o'clock struck a party was exactly what I needed: drink; the tranquillizing company of Sue; the stimulating company of Christopher. I didn't go and get these things because of the damned hysterical schoolboy I had been horrified, the evening before, to discover in myself: the shrill, joke-jealous lover. Lover? Well, that was the rub. I couldn't bear to make another exhibition of myself, and I feared, if I went, that I would. I couldn't bear to see Sue and Christopher enjoying things in each other's company: enjoying each other's company; and I knew, if I went, that I would. So I played at doing some more work and went early and dismally to bed.

Saturday morning I spent most unusually at the office. Saturday afternoon I spent partly in bed, partly doing some more work. Saturday evening I could have spent at Lavinia's peak-party, which she was giving jointly with Godfrey Peters, and to which she had asked me; but after a small dinner in my small nearby restaurant I went back to bed.

On Sunday I still had plenty of home-work to do, but very little energy to do it. I did nothing. I divided my time between an armchair and the sofa, trying to think about anything but Sue and Christopher and thinking, hour after hour, about Sue and Christopher. At half-past seven Victoria Crabbe surprised me by ringing up and asking me to come to the peak-party she was giving jointly with Angelica. I surprised myself by accepting.

"I know it's not part of the rules, your coming," she said, suggesting a high-bred disregard for rules, "but do come just the same."

"I'd love to, thank you very much."

I had been sitting still too long, that's what it was, so I was glad to go. In the first minute of arriving I was sorry I'd come. I saw, as I had hardly expected, Sue and Christopher. Christopher noticed me at once. He turned to say something to Sue; she nodded; he came towards me. I made to avoid him, but he caught me.

"Major, I insist that you listen to me."

"But—— "

"Oh come on."

"All right," I said, "all right."

"Come out here."

He led me out into the crimson-striped hall of the flat, and then (since this hall was rather a thoroughfare) up to a small landing. For the next quarter-hour I realized what it really meant to be talked to like a Dutch uncle: Christopher talked to me like one. It doesn't matter what he said. The thing is, I believed him. So I went down and took Sue's hand and spoke to her and she smiled. It was in order that this should happen that Christopher had asked Victoria to ask me that evening, and had asked himself, and had brought Sue. Christopher was that kind of friend.

When we were all three talking together quietly (Cristopher having, after a delicate interval, rejoined Sue and myself) I began for the first time to notice the rest of the party. It was awful. The I. girls were there in force, talking in high-pitched voices about cultural matters and next week's parties. Among them, standing in courtly attitudes, were a number of very terrible young men. These young men fell into two categories of about equal size: those who, having taken the Foreign Office examination and passed, were now in the Foreign Office and loving it; and those who, having taken the Foreign Office examination and failed, were now in Lloyds and pretending to hate it. I felt old and scruffy among them, though I was nearly the same age and wearing nearly the same clothes. Christopher looked twice the size of any of them: a member he seemed, of a different, more heroic race. I knew most of them, and some of them knew me. Christopher knew them all. Sue didn't know any of them, and didn't want to. Godfrey Peters didn't know any of them either, and wanted to terribly.

Poor Godfrey: I felt sorry for Godfrey. He dimmed, that evening, among the smarties: dimmed and disappeared. I don't think Lavinia ever saw him again. (Sue told me afterwards that she had felt sorry for him too, and in the same way, so she had asked him to dinner. He had told her— perhaps absent-mindedly, since she knew the facts—a great deal of gossip about Lavinia which suggetsed (*a*) that he knew her very well indeed and had probably had an affair with her, and (*b*) that he'd firmly broken with her for reasons he was not at liberty to divulge. She stopped being sorry for him after that. I stopped after thirty seconds, because other things were claiming my attention.)

"We've got a new concept," one of the diplomats was saying, "a wonderful new concept."

"Oh, *Philip*— " giggled Angelica.

"But it's wonderful, you must hear about our new concept. It's no less than a code for I.G. behaviour!"

"Really?"

"Yes. It's called the 'Concept of Inadmissability'. It pro-

71

vides an absolutely certain way of knowing whether some-one is I.G. or not, even in the most subtle borderline cases. In the first instance, you can tell a man's not I.G. by some particular thing he does—some Non-I.G. indicator phrase he uses, or some kind of trousers he wears—— "

"Yes, I can see that."

"Well, he's out at once, d'you see, a clear case. But there are near-I.G.s, aren't there—people you can't tell about at once—people you're never quite sure about?"

"*I* can always tell—— "

"Nonsense, Angie, you can't possibly. But by the correct application of the concept of inadmissibility you can tell absolutely for certain. What you do is, you find out if your candidate *realizes* that things are inadmissible, and what things. Take an obvious inadmissible. Take the most ob-vious. Take having badges on the front of your car—— "

"Rows of badges? Clubs and things?"

"Yes. Well, note the two stages. You have your chap who has rows of badges on the front of his frightful sports-car—"

"Inadmissible. Non-I.G."

"Just so. That's stage one. Then you have your chap who has no badges. Right, may be I.G., may not. Perhaps he belongs to the R.A.C. and he's just lost his badge. Perhaps he normally has *thirty* badges and he just happens to be having them all cleaned. Perhaps, more subtly, he doesn't actually like badges, but he has no sort of thing against them—he could easily, if he happened to like them, imagine himself with any number."

"I *see*. Philip, it's *mar*vellous."

"Yes," said Philip complacently, "it's quite useful."

I said to Christopher: "I'm inadmissible."

"I fancy so," he agreed.

"Smoking pipes," Victoria was saying.

"Saying 'old boy'."

"Carrying a swizzle-stick."

"Yes, and *calling* it a swizzle-stick."

"What do you call it?"

"A champagne-whisk, Victoria," said Philip austerely.

"Inadmissible tastes," said a man called Tim. "Brahms. Cézanne. Thackeray."

"Shelley. Gainsborough."

"Handel. Vanbrugh. Michaelangelo."

"Inadmissible things to be," said a man called Henry Fenwick, an unhappy young man who could have been nice but wasn't, at the moment, nice at all. "A naval officer. A doctor. A don."

"A red-brick don, yes."

"Any don."

"Some dons are I.G., Henry, let's face it—— "

"Well, a few young ones. Most inadmissible of all, saying 'let's face it'."

"Well, yes. It slipped out."

"Aren't you Townsend?" said a harsh voice behind us.

"Yes," said Christopher, turning. An aquiline grey-haired man in a shaggy tweed suit was leaning by the fireplace. "Thought I knew you. My name's Hallowes."

"Of course, sir. Er, this is Miss Susan Chase, Mr. Melot, Sir Hilary Hallowes."

"How do you do?"

"What are you doing now, boy?"

"I've just started working for my godfather, Jonathan Cornish—— "

"*Have* you, *have* you? Able fellow, Cornish."

"I've always admired him immensely," agreed Christopher gravely.

"Ah. I make advertisements of a kind myself—— "

That was why the name was familiar: Hapgood and Hallowes Ltd., Screen Advertising.

"Of course, sir," I said. "I've seen a lot of your films."

"Terrible stuff, most of it—— "

"Oh no, far from it—— "

"Well," he chuckled coldly, "I don't really think so myself."

"Are you in the Everest Club, Sir Hilary?" asked Sue, voicing my own surprise.

He chuckled again, less coldly. "Little Victoria—she's my secretary, d'you know her?—yes, you would of course—she pulled me into it. Amuses me in a way."

"Amuses us in a way," said Christopher, waving at the room.

"No, my dear," came a clipped voice, "no *no*, Angie. I assure you that grey-flannel trousers unless *very dark indeed* are quite inadmissible."

"In a way is right," I said, suddenly irritated.

"Stupid young wasters," said Sir Hilary in his disagreeable voice. "Look at those trousers—— "

"I agree with you about the trousers," said Christopher untruthfully.

"I don't know that I agree with you about the stupid," I said. "Silly, I'd say, but surely not stupid?"

"Nonsense," he said, his hot blue eyes staring at me arrogantly from either side of his thin nose. I began to dislike Sir Hilary. "Stupid," he repeated. "I *know* people."

"A business like yours, sir," said Christopher tactfully.

"Quite. I've been taking people on and paying them and sacking them, by God, for thirty years, and—— "

I had an uncontrollable desire to talk to Sue privately for a few minutes. I had nothing to say: I just wanted to talk to her privately. There was no reason why I should control this desire, so I indulged it: we talked in happy whispers in the crimson-striped hall for two or three or it may have been ten minutes.

When we came back into the party—having empty glasses

and no need, yet, for solitude—Christopher and the bullying old man were still talking by the fireplace behind the starling chatter of the I. girls and their court.

"Sir Hilary's looking for a television director," said Christopher. "He hoped to find one among Victoria's clever friends."

"I doubt," I said, "if you'll find any sort of TV man in this bunch, sir."

"I don't want what you call a TV man. Last thing I want is some half-baked poop from the B.B.C. who's looking for bigger money in commercial work, and who'll always think he's prostituted his talent by making advertising commercials. I know the sort of trained professional you mean. I doubt if he'd last a fortnight with me." He stared at me fiercely again, staring me down. He had no difficulty doing this: I was glad to look away. "Want to know the sort of man I'm looking for?" he went on. "A genius. Think that's a tall order? Think I won't get one? Don't believe there is such a thing, perhaps?" He dared me to think there wasn't such a thing. "I'll find one all right, take it from me. I always find what I want. That's what my competitors hate about me." He chuckled again—the horrible self-assured chuckle of a successful bully. "I want a man who can think big. Then I can talk to him. I want a man with ideas and imagination and no blasted so-called professional training to put blinkers over his eyes. Then I can use him. I want a man—— "

This boring monologue was interrupted by a nervous cough from beside us. "Excuse me," said a young insurance broker politely, "that ashtray behind you, sir—— "

Sir Hilary expelled a long, long-suffering sigh. "I'm try-ing," he said, "to talk. Know that word, young man? T-A-L-K."

"Oh sorry," stammered the broker, "sorry—— "

"I think, sir," I said, "I wonder—— "

75

"What?"

"Christopher, do you think Sir Hilary ought to meet Perkins?"

"Perkins!" exclaimed Christopher. "That's a very good idea. Perkins, sir, is a man we know a little and admire a lot—— "

"What does he do?"

"He's a novelist," I said, "and a philosopher."

"Successful?"

"Not yet, no."

"Good. Cheaper, then, ha ha."

"Ha ha."

"He's certainly original," said Christopher. "A near-genius, I think I'd call him."

"Ooh," cried Sue, "*near*-genius? I think Mr. Perkins is certainly a genius. Well, if he isn't I'd like to know what is—"

"I think Sue's right," I said. "Perkins has got extraordinary grasp and vision—— "

"Hm," grunted Sir Hilary. "Got his address?"

"I'll ring you up with it in the morning, sir, if you like."

"Do. Give it to my secretary. Well, good night, Townsend. Give my regards to Cornish." He nodded brusquely to me, ignored Sue, elbowed his way through the exquisites, barked a farewell to Victoria, and disappeared.

"What a horrid man," said Sue.

"He'll have fun with Perkins."

"Poor Perkins."

"Oh, I don't think so," I said. "Perkins won't notice anything. He might even get the job."

"*What?*"

"Oh yes," agreed Christopher. "Sir Hilary is very stupid."

"I don't see how he can be," said Sue. "He's terribly successful, isn't he?"

"Hapgood," explained Christopher, "his partner."

"Oh, I see—— "

"I'd love to be in on that interview."

"So would I."

"I'll die if Perkins gets that job."

"So will I. So will Perkins, if he's there for more than a week."

"Poor Perkins."

Three-quarters of an hour later Sue and I were in bed. Some time afterwards we were lying side by side and staring at the yellowish ceiling of her room.

"Will you marry me?" I said.

"Yes, darling," said Sue, "of course I will."

"Oh good."

"I do hope you really mean it, because I think it's a very good idea."

"So do I, now."

"You didn't before, did you?"

"Oh well, before. . . . No, not before."

"I don't think I did, before, either," said Sue comfortably, "but I jolly well do now."

So that was all right.

Presently she said: "One thing I must tell you. About your boss."

"Jonathan?"

"Yes. Do you know what I saw, coming out of a funny little house in Fulham yesterday afternoon?"

"Not Jonathan?"

"Yes. And do you know who with?"

"Fulham? I can't think."

"Clare Perkins."

"Good God."

"Darling, you *must* stop saying 'good God'—Clare, yes. Odd, I thought it."

77

"*Odd*—good God, Sue—I mean—— " we both laughed. "I mean, *Clare*. . . ."

"Odd," said Sue, "but not extraordinary, you know."

"I think it's the most extraordinary thing I ever heard. I mean, Jonathan and Clare—the thing's grotesque. Disgusting, if it weren't so absurd."

"Well, it's not quite like that really. We weren't quite right about Clare, last time we talked about her."

"What do you mean? Not a bitch?"

"Oh, a bitch, well. . . . No. She's got something, you know."

"Looks, yes—— "

"More than that. I was watching her at your flat the other evening—— "

"That awful evening."

"That awful evening. The thing is, she responds. *You* know what I mean. She reacts. Oh, she's definitely got something."

"Not for me."

"She's not your cup of tea, darling. Seems to be Jonathan's, though."

"Good God—— "

I told Jonathan, next morning, about Sue and me. He was delighted and charming about it.

"Oh *good*, Eddie, *good*. I saw Sue for a moment, as a matter of fact, on Saturday. She didn't see me."

"Yes she did," I said. "You were with Miss Perkins."

"That's right. Er, yes."

"Jonathan—— " I began. But the telephone rang, and then a client arrived unexpectedly, so we never finished the conversation. I expect Jonathan was relieved: I have never been any good at hiding my feelings—I haven't got that sort of face—and I daresay he saw what was in my mind. I know

I was relieved. I was terrified Jonathan was going to make a fool of himself—rich, middle-aged bachelor, tarty little bitch: it was a joke situation, a familiar farce situation, Pasquale, Falstaff—but how on earth could I find the words to tell Jonathan so? It was moral cowardice, but I was thankful that telephone rang, and thankful when plump Mr. Simpson of Belgravia Bond was ushered in by Lavinia.

On Thursday, three days later, I was Everest. Perkins had told me about being Everest. You sat in your flat all evening while people came from all over London with bags of half-crowns, or, at worst, rang you up to say they were sending cheques. This seemed a good way of spending the evening, and after dinner I was full of pleasurable anticipation.

It didn't, however, work out quite like that. What with the two large preoccupations of being busy and being in love, I had not done what the originators of the Everest Club sensibly recommended one did: watch the progress of one's descendants and ensure their satisfactory proliferation. The result was that I practically had no descendants. The thing had broken down nearly everywhere. We had, in fact, come in too late. Nobody came with bags of half-crowns. Nobody came with *any* half-crowns. There were, to be sure, some telephone calls. At ten a man rang up to say he was sorry, but he'd only got one great-grandchild and he thought he'd keep the half-crown himself. At ten forty-five a woman rang up to say she had three great-grandchildren and she was sending me a postal order for seven-and-six. She did, too. At eleven fifteen another woman rang up and promised fifteen shillings. This never arrived. At eleven thirty Christopher rang up to ask how much I had collected. I told him, and he roared with laughter.

"Shut up," I said. "It's most disappointing."

"My dear old Major, what *did* you expect?"

79

"Well," I admitted, "fifty pounds."

"Fifty *pounds*?"

"Yes, why not? It seemed to be going all right—— "

"You're potty."

"Well, yes—— "

"It never seemed to me to be going at all. Quite fun. Nice and zany. But *going*, no."

"No."

"I saw the most terrible play this evening."

"What?"

He told me. "I went in a large gloomy party," he continued, "and afterwards we had a large gloomy dinner in a large gloomy—— "

"Stop it," I said, "you're boring me."

"And myself," he agreed sadly. "But listen to this, Major, This is extraordinary. Do you know who I saw in the interval, lapping it up at the bar?"

"No?"

"Uncle Jonathan."

"That's not so extraordinary. Why shouldn't he go to the theatre? Quite nice people do—— "

"Yes, but listen. Do you know who he had with him, dolled up to the nines and looking, I must say, pretty good? Answer me that, you damned old *embusqué*."

"Clare," I said.

"Oh—— Yes."

"Oh dear," I said, "oh dear."

"Well, but," he said, "she looked pretty good."

"What's that got to do with it?"

"They were having fun."

"How could you possibly tell?"

"Of course I could tell. You can always tell."

"Well," I admitted, "yes, that's true. Did you talk to them?"

"Barely. I was involved with my large gloomy party, and God knows they were involved—— "

"With their tiny gay party?"

"Just so, Major. Just so, just so."

"Good God—— "

Four days later—Monday again—I was having lunch with a client who was also (like so many of our clients) an old friend of Jonathan's.

"Oh, by the way, Eddie," he said over the steak, "knew I had something to tell you. Fine bit of gossip. Horrifying. Know who I saw at Maidenhead on Saturday? In a boat?"

"Jonathan," I guessed sadly.

"How did you know? How *could* you know? How annoying of you to know—— "

"Oh well—— "

"But, my dear Eddie, with a popsie. Pretty girl, very. Little blonde. Envied him, I can tell you. They seemed— what's the word?—absorbed? Sunk?—— "

"Engrossed?"

"That's it. Engrossed in each other."

"Good God—— "

On Wednesday Jonathan and I had a long, late meeting with Mr. Simpson of Belgravia Bond, and when we had seen him into his taxi at a quarter to seven we decided to have a quick drink before we went back—as I thought we both had to—to our respective desks.

There was a nice little bar in the basement of our building where we gave clients drinks and, on occasions like this, ourselves drinks. Jonathan poured out two stiff ones and we sat heavily down in the small leather-covered chairs, holding our glasses greedily. We talked about Mr. Simpson and his problems for a few minutes. Then Jonathan swallowed his drink and said he must go.

"Golly," I said, "is the rush that bad?"

"I'm dining out this evening," he explained. "Meant to be picking someone up at eight. Got to change first."

He smiled a secret, inward-looking smile—the small smile people make when they cannot conceal their satisfaction, well-being, or glee. He looked quite as tired as I felt; we had had a far from satisfactory meeting; he had the evident beginnings of a bad cold. But he was on top of the world.

"Hm," he said, "hm. Well, good night, Eddie. Thank you very much for all your help this afternoon. See you in the morning. . . ." Still smiling, he went out.

Sadly I poured myself another big drink.

On the Friday of that week—the third week of September —I lunched again with Jonathan at Grey's. We were trying to persuade a client—a man who made jam—that he ought to use television advertising when it started. Christopher, as Television-Director-Designate, was also there. So were one or two other people who don't, mercifully, come into the story. So, near us in the dining-room, were the two old men whom Christopher had so dreadfully offended and so notably appeased a fortnight before. (They gave him a very courteous good day.) So also, near me in the cloak-room after lunch, were two middle-aged men collecting their hats and umbrellas. They were talking in low voices, but they were just the other side of a row of hanging coats and I couldn't help hearing what they said.

"—coming a cropper."

"Most unexpected. Last man in the world one would have thought of, to do a thing like that. Don't you think? More *sense*, you would have said."

"Oh well, sense. Doesn't apply. When a fellow of his age

—*our* age—goes off the deep end for a girl like that . . . sense, ha! Just doesn't apply."

"But, Frank, of all the men you and I know—— "

"I agree, I agree. Strange business, terrible. But there it is. Seen it before, see it again I daresay, and it makes you feel rotten every time."

Three weeks later the engagement was announced.

Chapter Five

✣

There it was, in *The Times*, on a grey Wednesday
morning of weeping skies and sad, uncertain light;
. . . *between Jonathan Mark, only son of the late
Brigadier-General and Mrs. John Cornish, of Fordings Hall,
Basingstoke, Hants, and Clare Margaret, daughter of Mr. and
Mrs. Claud Perkins, of 73 Lamancha Avenue, London S.W.6.*

Grossly shocking as it was to me, the progress of this improbable courtship hadn't really sunk into my mind. It had
been, all along, too awful to take seriously. I had been, all
along, working very hard for very long hours. I was myself
deeply in love and recently engaged and full of absorbing,
selfish wonder at this surprising and happy turn of events.
So seeing the announcement in cold print—how cold that
print was!—seeing the announcement there made me face
properly for the first time that Jonathan was taking Clare
Perkins to wife. I saw, for the first time, Clare as mistress of
Fordings. Clare as my Chairman's wife. Perkins, come to
that, as my Chairman's brother-in-law—Perkins, perhaps,
taken by unavoidable nepotism on to Jonathan's payroll.
Clare at the sort of business dinners where directors' wives
appear. Clare being nice to me and Clare condescending,
with Chairman's-wife affability, to Sue.

It was too awful. It was not to be borne.

I went and congratulated Jonathan soon after I got to the office. I couldn't be ecstatic, try as I might. I could only hope my moderate and insincere remarks were convincing. Evidently they weren't, altogether:

"Thank you, Eddie," said Jonathan, "thank you very much." Then he said: "You'll understand about Clare when you get to know her, which must be soon."

"Well, I certainly hope so—— "

"Yes. Well. I must say I thought I was set fair to being a bachelor for the brief evening of my days—— "

"I must say I thought so, too."

"What, at your age?"

"No, I mean about you."

"Ah. Well, placed as you are you'll know what I mean when I say how delighted I am at the prospect of not being a bachelor any longer. No way to be."

"Ha ha, no, absolutely not—— "

I was at once disturbed and reassured to see that Jonathan neither looked nor sounded like a love-struck middle-aged man under the chorus-girl spell of youth and fluttering eyelashes. He looked and sounded like a man in love but knowing exactly what he was doing and feeling thoroughly happy about it. But disturbed, it made me feel, yes: he is so totally besotted (I thought) that he doesn't realize he's besotted. He knows it's right and proper and normal to fall in love with people; he doesn't realize, being blinded, that it's all wrong and improper and disastrous for him to fall in love with a common little bitch like Clare.

"Well," I finally said, "I've got a lot of stuff to get back to—— "

"Poor Eddie, yes I know. Well—— "

On this unconvincing note I left, depressed and baffled, for my own room.

I met Christopher on the way.

85

"Come in," I said. "Can we have some coffee, Jacqueline, please? Well, Christopher—— "

"Well, Major—— "

"What do you make of this?"

"Make of it? What should I make of it?"

"You know what I mean. This ghastly business—— "

"Up to a point," he said, "I see what you mean. But I don't really want to hear your views, you know, not at any length."

"No. No, I suppose not—— "

"Dear Uncle Jonathan. I think he may be very happy."

"*Do* you? *Do* you, Christopher?"

"Yes, I do. Why not?"

"Well, Clare—— "

"She may have trouble with some of her vowel-sounds, Major, and she may do things to her hair we don't quite like, but she's quite a girl, you know. I don't think you see the point of Clare. She *is* quite a girl. Can you imagine Uncle Jonathan marrying anyone who wasn't?"

"I can imagine any middle-aged bachelor making—making a mistake. I mean, it's a well-known thing. As to Jonathan, well I admit it astounds me—— "

"Don't let it. Just don't let it. And it needn't. Clare's got something, you know."

"That's just what Sue said. But. . . ."

He nodded. "I expect she did. Sue's a great girl. Far too good for a silly, stuffy old Major who—— "

"I know. I know that. . . . But Christopher, what I honestly don't see is, what has Clare got? Can you see it? I mean, respect for Jonathan aside, can you really *see* it?"

"Oh yes. I'm not certain I can define it, but I can certainly see it, yes."

"I'm absolutely damned if I can. What is it?"

"Well," he pondered, "life. Drive. A kind of fierceness. She goes straight at things. I like that."

I could make nothing of this, and said so.

"It's the opposite kind of quality from Sue's," Christopher went on. "And Clare's the opposite kind of person—— "

"I'll say she is."

"—but she's got something, yes. Besides, Major, whether you see it or not, and what*ever* you *ever* think of Clare, it's Jonathan's business, you know."

"Yes. Oh yes, only—— "

"We shouldn't be talking about it like this."

"No."

"And anyway, you just don't know her. You've barely met her. You'll have to know her much better before you can judge. Before you even *can,* let alone *may*."

"Know her better—that's just what Jonathan said."

"Well, as I seem merely to be echoing the comments of everyone else, to continue this conversation is plainly useless. Useless," he stared at me seriously, "and improper."

He left, and I turned to the problems of selling zip-fasteners in selected export markets.

I did, of course, get to know Clare much better. But I never really understood what they all meant.

Nevertheless I did, as it were, join their camp almost immediately. This was Lavinia's doing.

"Oh Eddie," she said to me as I was on my way out to lunch, "isn't it ghastly?"

"You mean—— ?"

"You know what I mean. That awful little piece—— "

"Not G." I said.

"Oh, do you know that word? No, exactly, *not* G. And—— "

"I think," I said, "we really ought all to mind our own

87

business. Keep the concept of inadmissibility right out of this."

"Oh, do you know that too? How odd—Well yes, actually I suppose you're right, but really I can't help talking to you about it, Eddie, because I know you feel the same way I do——"

"Tell me later," I said. "I must go."

Most of Jonathan's friends took Christopher's view. Some took, in private, the view I had taken with Christopher, but in public the line I had taken with Lavinia. A few took Lavinia's view; notable among these, Christopher told me, was Jonathan's sister.

This sister was a widow in the middle forties called Mrs. Connell. Colonel Connell's photograph stood on a bookcase in the morning-room at For dings: a blurred, indeterminate face with a moustache that looked as though it must have been red. I only ever found out two things about the late colonel, in all the time I knew his widow, his brother-in-law, and his children: his relict always referred to him, on the rare occasions when she did so, as "my poor dear Gerald"; and a man I once sat behind on a bus in Oxford Street said to his companion "I was serving at the time under that stupid bastard Gerry Connell, and I nearly died of it."

Mrs. Connell had two children of school age, who were said to be coming into a lot of money at some point. She and they lived at Fordings with Jonathan. She kept house for him; he kept them. I heard her views about her brother's engagement early, because on the Thursday after the Wednesday of *The Times* announcement Jonathan asked me and Sue to stay for the week-end.

"Clare's coming," he said, "and I want you to meet her properly."

"I'll have to consult Sue," I said, "but as far as I know we'd love to come."

"My sister Millicent will be there, of course. You've met her, haven't you?"

"Yes indeed. Er, how is Mrs. Connell?"

"Very well, Eddie, thank you. Her children are at home too, at the moment."

"Oh? I thought it was term-time?"

"Well, it is. But Jeremy's school has got mumps, and Millicent has taken against Daphne's headmistress and has removed her."

"Oh, what a bore. For you, I mean. Or isn't it?"

Jonathan laughed. "All the letters you read in the newspapers from parents complaining that school holidays are far too long," he said, "I agree with."

"I haven't met the children—— "

"You will."

"Bad as that?"

"Well. . . . They're very well-behaved."

"That's something, surely? Almost everything, I would have thought."

"I *would* have thought so, too . . . I've got to go to a blasted dinner on Friday evening, by the way, so I'll be driving Clare down late. We'll arrive about midnight, I expect. If I were you I'd take the five fifty-five. I'll ring up and say you're coming, and someone'll meet you."

"Wonderful, Jonathan, thanks—— "

Duly, therefore, Sue and I disembarked stiffly into the dark bustle of Basingstoke station at seven o'clock that Friday evening. It was cold—the first really cold night of the year. All around us pressed bowler-hats and furs and cloth caps and sad checked coats; they carried us like pieces of cork towards the narrow, sternly guarded door marked

"Way Out". Under the cold yellow lamps warm steam hissed; warm breath puffed expansively out from many a glad and welcoming mouth.

"Hullo there, Mother!"

"Oh Henry, aren't you *late*?"

"No no, don't think so—— "

"Coo, isn't it cold?"

"Got the cases? *All* the cases? Where's my little case?"

"Come along old boy, this way, that's the style—— "

"Ticket, sir?"

"Ever so cold, Henry."

"Got a season somewhere—— "

"No no, the little case—oh, *really*, darling—— "

"Nippers all right, Mother?"

"Well, Doctor says—— "

"Car's round here old boy—had a devil of a job getting in—altogether too many cars about nowadays, absolute menace—— "

"Excuse me, that's my foot, excuse *me*—— "

"I declare I've lost my platform ticket—Henry, I say I've lost my platform ticket."

"Oh Mother, trust you—— "

"Any birds this year?"

"Not bad. Had a grand shoot last week, pity you weren't here—— "

"Brrr—not half cold—— "

"Excuse *me*, that's my elbow—— "

"No, *that's* not my little case—*you* know my little case—oh, darling, *really*—— "

"Jonathan's car is a Bentley," I told Sue. "Oldish. Black. Ought to be here somewhere."

"Could that be it?"

"That's it. Good."

"It's full of people."

"*Is* it? So it is. We'll go and see—— "

"Mr. Melot?"

"That's right. This is Mr. Cornish's car, then?"

"It is that, sir. *Here* we are. . . . These all your bags?"

"Yes, that's the lot. Back or front, Sue? All right, I'll go in the back—Hullo, are you the Connells?"

"Yes, sir."

"Yeth."

"You must be Jeremy and you must be Daphne."

"Yes, sir."

"Yeth."

"It's very nice of you to come and meet us on such a beastly cold night—— "

"Yes."

"Well! I hear you've got mumps at your school, Jeremy?"

"Yes, sir. Arbuthnot got them. They said he caught them in the cinema, p'raps, but I know why he got them."

"Why?"

"Because he *stole*."

"Oh—that's bad. . . ."

"Yes, sir. Stealing's a sin. He stole Meredith's sweets out of his play-box while Meredith was doing gym. That's a sin."

"And you think he got mumps as a punishment?"

"Yes, sir. No sin goes unpunished. The eye of the Most High sees everything we do. We have to be terribly careful, all the time."

"Yes, we do, don't we? How old are you, Jeremy?"

"Eleven, sir."

"Good God—— "

"Eddie—— " said Sue warningly.

"The Good God," I amended rapidly, "moves in mysterious ways—— "

"Yes, sir."

"Er, did you *see* what's-his-name pinch the sweets out of the other boy's play-box?"

"Yes, sir. I was watching him."

"What, purposely?"

"Yes, sir. I followed him to watch him. I wanted to be the instrument of the Lord, and I was."

"You mean you—— "

"I reported the offender to Mr. Inskip. He was caned."

"If he was caned it's a bit hard he got mumps too—— "

"Expiation for a sin against the Lord of Hosts isn't always granted at once. Mr. Inskip says so."

"Ah—— "

Sue turned round. "Are you going to go to another school, Daphne?"

"Yeth, I think tho."

"Mm. Did you like the other one?"

"No."

"Weren't the girls nice?"

"They weren't in a thtate of grathe."

"Oh—— "

"How old are you, Daphne?" I asked.

"Eight."

"Good God."

"Eddie—— "

But I couldn't be bothered this time.

"Oh, how do you do?" Mrs. Connell was saying presently. "How *do* you do? Well. You'll want to see your rooms, I expect—— "

Soon we were standing by a large wood fire in the lovely drawing-room. An obvious Guardi, a possible Canaletto, a large and grotesque Stubbs hung among the bookcases and windows, and a Reynolds dominated the room from over the fire. The remote, elegant Miss Cornish of the picture, for all her yellowish gloss and her heavy Georgian features, was easily the second most real women in the room. Her modern collateral hardly seemed to be there.

"A little more sherry," she fluted. "Ah—My brother Jonathan tells me I neglect people's glasses, and I fear it is true. I never drink more than a small half-glass myself, my head is so weak. But then——"

"Then?"

"Oh—— " She fluttered away, with thin grey hands, the need to finish her remark. Thin and grey, that was Mrs. Connell, and she seemed, like the lady of the picture, to have an old cracking coat of yellowish varnish.

"My brother Jonathan tells me he will arrive about midnight," she said. "So dreadfully late. I'm afraid Miss Perkins will be tired."

"Yes, I expect she will be, rather."

"We must see that she has a restful time at Fordings. . . . You have met my prospective sister-in-law, Mr. Melot?"

"Yes indeed. 'Met' is about it, actually—I've really hardly spoken to her for more than a moment."

"Ah, well, after all—— "

"Mm?"

Again she waved away, with moth-like hands, the need for explanation.

"It was very nice to meet your children, Mrs. Connell," said Sue.

"Ah, how kind of you to say so. . . . Well. Jeremy is so sad to miss this term, it's the one he most enjoys."

"Oh, he likes football?" I was surprised.

"No no, he is far too delicate, I am afraid, for football."

"Oh—— "

"What very religious children they are, Mrs. Connell."

"Oh, I hope so." Her pale eyes were shining. "I do rejoice they are. My poor dear Gerald was a deeply religious man, and I am so thankful his children take after him."

"Yes, yes indeed." I had intended a mild joke about schoolchildren's religion, but I abandoned the idea.

"Dinner is served, madam," said the pleasant man who had brought us from the station, now appearing black-coated in the door.

"Ah, dinner, I expect you're very hungry—all that way on such a dreadful night—— "

"I'm famished," said Sue.

"Oh dear, I do hope there'll be enough—— "

There was: it was an excellent meal—a shade pretentious, like everything at Fordings, but all the better (I felt) for that.

We went back to the drawing-room for coffee. Mrs. Connell's manner of pouring coffee was different from other people's. Instead of a continuous black stream from spout to cup she produced little nervous spasms of coffee, some of which spilled into each of the three successive saucers.

"I'm so sorry," she gasped, "I seem to have spilt it most dreadfully—would you like me to ring for fresh saucers, it might be best. . . ."

"No no, certainly not, please don't trouble," I said heartily. "We can easily pour it back—it's only a drop."

"Oh—I'm so concerned that you may drip some on your trousers, or you, Miss Er, on your skirt. . . . My brother Jonathan tells me I should pour more courageously, but I scarcely know what he means. . . . Speaking of my brother Jonathan, I wish you would tell me about my future sister-in-law?"

"You probably know much more about her than I do," I said evasively. "I've hardly met her, you know—— "

"Oh, no—— "

"What?"

"I mean," she said helplessly, "I mean, one or two friends

of mine have written from London, very kindly, to tell me about Miss Perkins. Written most *oddly*— "

"Oddly?"

"Yes. One friend, a Miss Penfold, writes that Miss Perkins is really *not quite a lady*, which I cannot bring myself to believe can be true— "

"Oh well," I hedged.

"It depends where you draw the line," said Sue.

"Oh! What a curious point of view—how modern. . . . I'm afraid I'm dreadfully old-fashioned and out of the world, but it seems to me a very lamentable thing that Fordings should have as its new mistress a common young woman— "

"Well, yes, er— "

"One hates to think of children inheriting all this who are not quite—oh dear, I'm afraid I shouldn't be talking like this, my brother Jonathan would be quite offended if he could hear— "

"Oh well— "

She fluttered above the coffee-pot. "One can't help feeling the whole thing is a disaster."

I glanced at her with some sympathy, since she was voicing my own views exactly, and saw that her faded myopic eyes were harder than I should have thought possible.

"My own poor little two— "

"I gathered that they were, er, well provided for— "

"Fatherless," she murmured. "And quite what *I* shall do— "

"Well— "

"It's a terrible thing when a middle-aged man like my brother Jonathan—well, he could have married any number of respectable girls once, ladies, friends of mine—I had so many friends once—oh dear— "

"Oh— "

"And to become infatuated, well, one may as well come out with it, ensnared—— "

"Oh come, Mrs. Connell," said Sue mildly, "you haven't even met Clare yet. Do you think it's quite fair to judge her—— "

"Oh dear, *judge*, I wouldn't dream——'" she waved, with perilous helplessness, among the Crown Derby cups.

Sue and Mrs. Connell both went up early. I was very tired: but my armchair was comfortable; the fire was at the perfect glowing point; the man-servant (Jonathan avoided, nowadays, the word "butler") had brought me, unasked, a decanter of whisky and a soda syphon; and I had found on a small table a new novel I wanted to read. So I told them I would read a little before I went to bed myself, and perhaps wait for Jonathan and Clare to come.

At twenty past twelve I heard a crunch outside the drawing-room windows: Jonathan's Mercedes. I expected to hear, immediately, doors slam as they left the car; footsteps on the gravel; voices. But there was dead silence after the car stopped. I went to the far window and parted the heavy curtains. The car stood by the front door with the inside light on; Jonathan and Clare were kissing passionately in the front seat. I let the curtain drop back and sank again into my chair, finishing my drink and lighting a cigarette.

Presently I heard the front door open, and I went out into the hall. Clare came in alone; a new crunch of wheels told me that Jonathan was putting the car away into the coach-house behind the house.

"Oh, hullo, Eddie," she said. I hadn't been sure that she knew my name; I was quite sure that she had never called me by it before.

"Hullo, Clare. Have a good drive down?"

"Wonderful. That car goes like the wind."

"Yes, it's a very good car—— "

She was wrapped in a big camel-hair coat with a high collar. Her bright fair hair was rumpled, as well it might be after what I had just seen. Her colour was high and she looked excited. Too high; too excited; too vivid and vivacious and declamatory and obvious altogether, she looked to me.

"Come into the warm," I said.

"Lovely—— "

Jonathan came in a moment later. He was wearing a white tie under his dark overcoat, and he looked tired and happy and ridiculously distinguished.

"Hullo, Eddie, how nice that you're still up."

"I was too comfortable to move. Your sister and Sue both went to bed hours ago."

"Sensible women. Is that whisky? Darling, have some whisky."

"Well—yes. I must say I'd love some. A little. Oh no—stop!—really a little—— "

"Really?" I thought. I could have sworn I'd heard her make it "reely" on one of those peculiar Everest evenings. How odd.

"Oh how nice", she murmured, stretching one hand to the dying fire. Jonathan smiled at her with infinite tenderness. Embarrassed, I threw my cigarette into the fire, said good night, and retreated.

After lunch the next day I was walking with Sue in the small walled garden behind the stables.

"What do you think of Clare now?" I asked her.

"What I thought before. She's got something. A lot."

"Oh. . . . You know, a most extraordinary thing, I could have sworn she had an accent before. Like Perkins's. A sort of cockney twang."

97

"Yes, she did."

"Well, I can't hear it now, I must say. Extraordinary—— "

"Is it? Such a good thing, I should have thought."

"Oh well, yes, for Jonathan—she's certainly getting herself assimilated quickly."

"Yes, she's clever. One up to her."

"In a way—— "

"She's changed her hair, too, have you noticed?"

"Oh, is that it? I thought she looked different."

"Very different, darling. Very different and *very* pretty."

"You're very pro-Clare all of a sudden," I said.

"Yes I am. That's partly because of you, actually, and partly because of our kind hostess, but mostly because of Clare."

"I'm not pro-Clare."

"Oh well, you. It's odd of you. I'm not sure, though, that I'd want you to be *very* pro-Clare—— "

After a pause I said: "She's learning *too* fast. There's something wrong in that."

"What *do* you mean?"

"Well, it's all part of it. It's sort of—sly. She's too—— " I groped "—too *sharp*."

"No, that's not quite the word."

"What is the word, darling?"

She thought. "Vital."

"Cant word," I said, "magazine fiction."

"That's easy to say. Though I see what you mean. But as a couple, after all, they *look* like the most *drivelling* magazine fiction."

"Jonathan, yes, every time. But she's not a beauty. Pretty, yes. Hard, rather—— "

"You're quite wrong, darling. She's lovely."

"Not to me."

"Good. But you're wrong, just the same."

"I don't see it. I just don't see it. Well. I suppose Jonathan is doing a kind of Pygmalion."

"Yes, I should think so. Sent her to French or someone. Chooses her clothes, perhaps. Jolly sensible."

"Jolly lucky for her, by God."

"Oh Eddie *darling*, are you switching from 'good God' to 'by God'? I don't believe I could bear it."

"Sorry," I said, "I do try—— "

At tea Sue said to Clare: "I do like the way you've got your hair now. It's new, isn't it?"

"Yes, it is. Thanks awfully. I didn't realize how terrible the other way was until I saw myself with it done like this."

Clever girl, I thought. Too clever by half.

"Oh, is that new?" said Jonathan. "So it is."

"*Really* Jonathan," I said jovially.

"I know, Eddie, it's shameful, but you must realize I'm only just beginning to learn about these things. Clare has to tell me when she's wearing something I haven't seen before, so I can make the right noises."

"You're improving," said Clare. "You noticed this suit without being told to."

They smiled at each other.

"We were wrong," I said.

"Yes," Sue agreed, "but I wasn't as wrong as you were."

After dinner I found myself with Mrs. Connell in a corner of the drawing-room. She had lost her pen, and I was trying to help her find it in the drawers of a table where old playing cards and balls of string were kept.

"I do so want to write a letter this evening," she said unhappily, making little futile digs into jumbles of string.

"Urgent?"

"Not really—*please* don't bother, oh dear, you are kind—No, I want to write a sharp letter to Isabel Penfold."

"I don't think I know——"

"No? Oh. . . . She wrote to me from London, kindly as I thought, about my brother Jonathan's engagement——"

"Oh, Miss Penfold, yes, you told us——"

"—with some horrid scurrilous remarks about dear Clare."

"Oh——"

"Such a sweet child. Do you know, she spent nearly the whole afternoon playing rounders with Jeremy and Daphne? It can't have amused her. They were so thrilled and grateful——"

"Yes, I'm sure——"

"And, do you know, Isabel Penfold distinctly says in her letter that dear Clare is not quite a lady. *Well!*"

We looked across the room. Jonathan was telling Sue and Clare about the horse in his large Stubbs.

"—and the awful thing was, it never actually won a race."

Sue giggled.

"Poor horse," said Clare.

Clare was wearing a black dress, very simple, without any jewellery except her engagement ring. Sue, beside her, looked almost fussy: though simply dressed, God knows, she was wearing ear-rings and a necklace and had a shawl round her shoulders.

"Such an elegant child," said Mrs. Connell, beaming mildly across the room at Clare. "And your *fiancée* so pretty, too, Mr. Melot."

"Yes, yes indeed——"

"Well well . . . I *must* find this pen—oh dear, how dreadfully absent-minded I am becoming—I shall be quite tart with Isabel."

Chapter Six

✤

The four of us went back on Sunday evening in Jonathan's Mercedes—his new London car. Jonathan was a very good driver and his driving was like himself: dashing, but without flamboyance. He used his beautiful rich-sounding horn very little; he waved pedestrians over zebra-crossings; he overtook everything.

The weather was horrible. After two fine days full of the first brilliant snap of winter it was warm and pouring. The wipers swung with mesmeric regularity left-right left-right over the windscreen; the wet road hissed under the tyres; on the side windows of the back seat, where Sue and I sat cosily bundled, large incessant drops of water zigzagged crazily across the glass from the top front corners to the bottom rear corners.

As we swung out of the roundabout from the Staines road into A 4 Clare twisted round. "When are you two getting married?"

"Next week," said Sue. "Friday."

"*What?*"

"My dears," said Jonathan, "I'd no idea it was so soon."

"Well, we couldn't see any point in waiting," I said.

"No no, quite right—— "

"Can we come?"

"Of *course*. Registry Office, I'm afraid."

"Like us," said Clare.

"Oh, are you too?"

"My parents don't approve of Church weddings. Even if they did it'd be Chapel."

"Oh—— "

"Are you having a reception, Sue?" asked Jonathan. "My *dear* fellow," he gently reproved an enormous lorry which had lurched across into the centre lane as we hissed past.

"Well," said Sue, "yes. Just. My parents—— "

"Are they coming?"

"Oh yes. They're a tiny bit put out about it all—they think it's frightfully sudden, and they've never even met Eddie, you see —— "

"Yes, I do see. Oh well. . . . So we all come and drink champagne and you go off in Eddie's car—— "

"Yes."

"Where to?" said Clare. "Or aren't you telling?"

"Majorca."

"*Won*derful."

"I hope so. Where are you going?"

"All over the place," said Jonathan. "Mostly Naples and Sicily."

"Wonderful."

"We hope so."

Jonathan and Clare walking hand in hand in the shabby Neapolitan streets. Jonathan and Clare, when they came back, hand in hand at Fordings; in London; everywhere. My old friend Christopher, in the fullness of time, disinherited. A little half-Perkins, in the fullness of time, owning and running Fordings.

I shut my mind to these unattractive visions and stared at the jerkily rushing-and-loitering silver-lit drops on my window.

At nine o'clock on Tuesday evening I was sitting in Sue's armchair pretending to read the evening paper. Sue had gone out to get some cigarettes, telling me I was tired, which was true. I was waiting for her with tender, growing impatience: it was getting on for my bed-time, I felt, and besides I wanted a cigarette.

The telephone rang. "Hullo?"

"Er, isn't that Miss Chase's number?"

"Yes, it is."

"Oh, is that you, Eddie? This is Clare."

"Oh hullo Clare, how are you?"

"Very well, thank you. I really wanted to talk to Sue—— "

"Sue's out just at the moment, I'm afraid. Any message?"

"Well, I wondered if both of you could come to a small sort of party at my parents' house on Thursday—it's a sort of—well, it's really so my family can meet Jonathan."

"Thursday, er, yes, I'm sure we can—— "

"Oh *good*."

"If you're quite sure," I said uneasily, "that you really want strangers in on a family affair—— "

"Oh yes. You see, Jonathan doesn't know many people like my family—well, I don't suppose you do, either—and I think he'll enjoy himself more if there are some of—some of the sort of people he's used to there—— "

This fogged me. "Oh, yes, well, fine. What sort of time?"

"Six."

"Ah. Well, we may be a bit late, if that's all right—drink-time is fairly elastic, though, isn't it, ha ha—— "

"Oh—well, it's not exactly a drinks-party, you know. Tea, really."

"Tea?"

"High tea."

"Oh I see. . . . We'd better be punctual, then."

"Well, if you *can*—— "

"Right," I said heartily, "right. Well. Thanks very much. I'll tell Sue as soon as she comes in. I'm sure we can come. Shall I ask her to ring you up, just in case?"

"You can't, I'm afraid. I'm calling from a box. We haven't got a telephone."

"Oh. Oh, I see. Oh well then—— "

"How very nice of her," said Sue when I told her.

"Does it strike you like that, darling? Personally I'm dreading it."

"So is she, poor sweet, obviously."

"Yes, I bet she is."

"Another one up to her, this is."

"I can't think how you make that out."

"*Can't* you? Well (*a*) she's showing us her family, who are obvisouly intensely shaming from her point of view—— "

"Well, yes. There is that."

"—and (*b*) she's trying to see that Jonathan has a good time."

"Do you think that's it?"

"Why not? Why shouldn't that be it?"

"Oh, well—— "

We were punctual on Thursday, but not as punctual as the rest of the party. We arrived at five past six; as we came into the Perkins's small sitting-room Clare introduced us, working clockwise round the room. The family, a dozen strong, were arranged about Jonathan in stiff attitudes in or behind chairs; all extended a hand and said that they were pleased to meet us. There were Clare's parents—he was a schoolmaster; Mrs. Perkins's sister and her husband—they kept an ironmonger's shop in Lewisham; Mr. Perkins's sister, unmarried—also a teacher; a grandmother in black;

three indeterminate youths; a family of cousins from High-bury.

I talked to Mr. Perkins.

"I gather from my daughter that you are a colleague of, er, Jonathan, Mr. er," he said.

I admitted this.

"I must, of course, deplore the nature of my prospective son-in-law's profession—— "

"Why?"

"—being as it is entirely concerned with the propagation of half-truths and untruths—— "

"Oh, I don't think that's quite fair—— "

"*Fair?*" His colourless short-sighted eyes stared at me angrily. "*Fair?* The purpose of commercial advertising is to make desirable to working-class housewives the apparatus of upper middle-class life. The people next door have television—we must. The Jones's have a washing-machine—we must. To *arrive*, to be *smart*," he glared at me, "you must bleach your hair or wear a more expensive coat that does not repel the rain nearly so effectively. So people whose weekly wage-packets barely suffice for the necessities of food, clothing, rent—these people mortgage months, even years, of wages in hire-purchase agreements for useless, damaging luxuries—— "

"Useless? Damaging?"

"—which are intended to give them the comfortable illusion that they are prosperous—that the country is prosperous—that an iniquitous mal-distribution of wealth and opportunity is inevitable or even desirable—— "

"Isn't the country prosperous?"

"Are old-age pensioners prosperous? Am I prosperous? You are, Mr. er, and my future son-in-law is, and" he said bitterly, "it appears that I must now rejoice that my daughter is to be so too—— "

"Yes."

"When she puts on her diamonds and her furs—— "

"Don't you want her to have diamonds and furs?"

"Do you know how many meals a diamond bracelet could buy?"

"Er—— "

"How many hours of teaching? How much treatment for a tubercular child?"

"Er—— "

He sniffed and went out to help his wife in the kitchen. I found myself talking to the grandmother.

"I'm so glad for Clarey," she said, "she's always been such a sweet child, so bright and sharp, why you'll be cutting yourself one of these fine days you will I said, you're so sharp, and she came right back at me, Granny she says, but Granny you'll put some plaster on if I do, won't you? she says, quick as a flash, well, that was when she was quite a tiny, but she's always been bright and cheery, always a cheery word, such a help about the house too, not like *some*—— "

"Oh?"

"—well that brother of hers, Adrian they call him—— "

"Oh yes, I know him—— "

"*Adrian*, well I said at the time, at the christening that was, if that's your idea of a name for a working boy well I don't know, I said, really and truly I don't—— "

"No, well—— "

"—but Clarey, yes, I'm ever so pleased and thankful she's getting a husband in a nice way of business, such a pleasant young man too, well not so young I daresay but what's a little difference in age? Nothing, and so I said to Claud— that's my son, Claud, you've just been talking to—I said love's love I said, I told him straight, love's love and you can't deny that—— "

"No indeed—— "

"—and if Clarey has a bit more money and gets to be grand and smart, well if she has a nice time isn't that what we should all wish her?—— "

"Yes, indeed—— "

"That's what I say to Claud. Charity begins at home, I say to him, and if you don't wish your daughter's happiness what sort of father are you? That's what I say."

The old lady rattled on and I looked about the narrow room. Sue was closely involved with the three youths; she was talking desperately and eliciting brief, muffled comments about recent American films. Jonathan was listening with grave interest to the vicissitudes of ironmongery in Lewisham. The family from Highbury were staring bitterly at Jonathan, at Clare, at Sue, at me, and whispering to each other through tight little mouths.

Presently we were sitting down in extravagant discomfort and eating sardines on toast and slices of bread and butter; it was rather enjoyable. I found myself sitting beside Clare's school-teacher aunt: a brisk, faded woman of fifty with a humorous face and fragile gold-rimmed glasses.

"You work with Jonathan, don't you?"

"Yes."

"Funny job it must be; or not?"

"Very funny, Very interesting."

"Yes, I expect so, like mine."

"Oh? Your brother doesn't, er, seem to approve of our trade—— "

"Oh, Claud, no he doesn't. No more do I. I'm not quite as fierce about it as he is—I'm not quite as fierce about anything as he is, though I usually agree with him in a general way—— "

"Ah—— "

"Still, I've got nothing but admiration for my niece. She's always known just what she wanted—money, glamour, class

—all the things this family's never had. Certainly can't blame her really. And now here she is going the best possible way about getting them all."

"Yes. That's about it."

She looked at me curiously. "You're as much against this as my brother is."

"Well—— "

"I'm a teacher. I've spent nearly thirty years seeing what people are thinking and I'm quite good at it. I know exactly what *you 're* thinking, and I don't know that I can really blame you, either. Your point of view's a special one and dear knows I don't share it, but I do see it—— " She laughed mildly. "Shall I tell you what my real attitude to Clare's engagement is? Remember that I'm a life-long Socialist and I'm completely against everything that Jonathan is and does—— "

"You must disapprove dreadfully."

"Part of me does. The rest of me just sits and envies."

"Oh—— "

She laughed again. "What do you expect an old spinster to feel? I teach English and I don't read women's magazines —I haven't the time and I haven't the taste for the stuff they print, But—— "

"But?"

"But how do you expect someone like me from a family like mine to react to cars and country houses and jewels and wine. . . . Do you know, I have never in my life drunk wine?"

"Oh—— "

"Never had the chance. No one's ever drunk wine in this family. Or anything else. Baptist, we were all brought up. Very strict. Blue Ribbon. We call ourselves agnostics now but we're still Baptists at heart. Claud is. I am. Drinking wine as a natural thing, just casually—you can't imagine how wicked and exciting that seems to me. It just seems wicked to Claud, and it just seems exciting to our mother (you were talking to her, weren't you? listening, rather, I expect), but with both together I get the best of both worlds—far the best attitude to young Clare's engagement—— "

"Even with envy?"

"Oh, envy's one of the pleasantest of the seven deadly sins. Anyhow it's about the only one I can still commit. The only one I ever *have* committed, come to that—— "

"Oh—— "

She laughed. "Have some more sardines? No? Nor will I. But I would like some more tea, if you can reach it—— "

I leant apologetically across a Highbury cousin (she looked at me with malevolence) and lifted the large brown tea-pot. As I poured, the door bounced open and Perkins— *our* Perkins—appeared theatrically on the threshold.

He was a surprising sight. Gone was the tight, wrinkled blue suit in which I had always seen him, gone the blue-and-red-striped shirt, gone the scuffed brown shoes. He was now resplendent in a dark grey flannel suit of irreproachable cut, dark brown suède shoes, a heavy cream silk shirt, an Ascot tie. His broad pink face wore a brisk executive air. In one hand he held a large, very new, black zip-fastened brief-case; in the other hand he held a large, very new, black Anthony Eden hat.

"Ah there," he cried, embracing the room with a generous sweep of the hat, "ah there, everyone. Can't stay long. Just come from a conference. Just off to another. Just looked in for a second. Just—— "

"Fiddle-de-dee, boy" shrilled his grandmother, "you so grand with your Sir Hilarious you don't know your own family? Well I never, well well I never—— "

"Ah, Gran, all well? That's right, that's right—ah, Melot, how are you? And Cornish—Sir Hilary sent you his regards—— "

"Thank you," said Jonathan faintly.

"—and I don't know but what we may not be doing business together soon, eh? But never a word, never a word——"

"How's the book?" asked Sue politely.

"Book, dear lady? Ah, the book. No time for that now, alas. Up to my neck, I assure you, we all are, absolutely swamped with work—off to Paris tomorrow to commission some productions—off to New York next week to see the theatrical agents—conferences, dinners, conferences again."

A minute later he disappeared as suddenly as he had come, sped by the mute, bitter disapproval of his father, the silent laughter of his aunt, the reproachful cackle of his grandmother, the angry resentment of the Highbury cousins, the amazement of us all. An engine purred and roared outside; immediately a large, very new, black Mark VII Jaguar flashed away with a chauffeur at the wheel.

"Golly," said Sue.

A Highbury cousin sniffed.

"Whatever next," said his grandmother, "whatever next indeed, off he goes in his fine Rolls-Royce without so much as a by your leave——"

"'S a Jag, Gran," muttered one of the youths.

"—or a *with* your leave, and what I say now *as* always——"

"Yes," said Sue, "one up to Clare."

"I don't get it," I said. "I thought it was ghastly."

"Of course it was ghastly. That's the *point*."

"I just don't get it."

"Oh *darling* what a stick you are, why on earth do I love you?" She paused. "But what about our Perkins?"

"Certainly one up to him."

"Two up."

"Eight or ten."

"Sucks to Sir Hilary."

"Double sucks," I agreed. "Serve him right. Nasty old bully."

The following day week Sue and I were married at a Registry Office in Chelsea. It was a dismal little ceremony on a wet, very dismal afternoon. Very few people were there: a dozen of my friends; half a dozen of Sue's friends; Sue's parents (he a tall, remote, snuffly G.P. who almost, but not quite, expressed his detestation of the whole affair; she a small woman with a faded fair prettiness who moved in an envelope of protective vagueness and talked of roses and bridge-scores); Christopher; Jonathan; Clare. Thankfully Sue and I left our drab little reception in a Kensington hotel and disappeared from England and from this story for three golden weeks.

PART TWO

Winter in Delirium

Winter in Delirium

✤

"**M**y dear Eddie, how glad I am to see you back. Did you have a good time?"

"Wonderful, thank you, Jonathan."

"Splendid to see you, Major. How *red* you are—— "

"Brown, I thought, more."

"—never have you looked so fully worthy of your majority. A scarlet major at the base—— "

"It's providential you're back, actually, Eddie, hideous as you no doubt find it—— "

"Oh well—— "

"—but we are slap in the middle of—— "

"*Spang*, my dear Major, in the middle of—— "

"Shut up, Christopher. Right in the middle of a crisis."

"A crisis—that's nothing new."

"This crisis is new." Jonathan paused. "Television."

"So soon?"

"None too soon. We're just about to make sixty experimental commercials, and—— "

"Good God."

"Dear old Major, how little marriage has changed that simple military soul—— "

"Sixty, though—— "

"Well, the experiment wouldn't be any good, we felt, unless it was comprehensive. The idea is to use as many different sorts of techniques as we possibly can, and see what they look like for our clients in our markets. Even dotty ideas, we ought to try—— "

"Yes, I see—— "

"—to explore, if you follow me, Eddie, as many paths as we can see even the slightest hope of our ever wanting to go down."

"We might show him the provisional list, Uncle Jonathan."

"Oh yes, good idea. Here we are. This is a list, you see, of the techniques we want to play about with. We've got live playlets, live demonstrations, pure entertainment filmlets with a selling twist at the end, ballet—— "

"—'Jingles,'" I read, "'sung spots, close harmony, *sprechgesang*' (are you serious about that one?)—— "

"We don't know yet. It's a path."

"To explore down, ye-es . . . 'Cartoon animation, pack animation, puppets (string and glove)'—the Klondykes, Christopher—— "

"We're in touch with them. They're rather good."

"Golly. 'Stop motion'—what the hell's that?"

"I must admit I'm not quite clear. You explain, Christopher."

"Well, I thought we might explain it all at H. and H. this afternoon, if the Major can come along—— "

"Eddie *must* come along. Can you, Eddie?"

"Of course. H. and H.? Hapgood and Hallowes?"

"Yes, we're making nearly all of these with them. All except the animation ones. These are all *films*, of course, you understand that—— "

"But to be used, when the time comes, on television?"

"Yes. H. and H. have got a new studio and a new department for this special thing—we think it'll be very useful —— "

"Good God. Perkins!"

"Well, yes. He does come into it—— "

"Good God."

"You're *back*, Mr. Melot!"

"Hullo, Jacqueline. Yes. Er, how are you?"

"Very well, thanks— *well*, at least, no, I've not been awfully grand—— "

"Oh—I'm sorry to hear that."

" —my *legs*—— "

"Oh dear."

" —and my *eyes*—— "

"Oh dear—glasses, perhaps?"

"Glasses, certainly not! Oh dear me, Mr. Melot, whatever next, *glasses*, what a fright I'd look. . . . Oh by the way—— "

"Oh, you've—— "

" —you haven't said—— "

" —changed you hair style, Jacqueline, haven't you? *Very* nice, that, I must say, suits you awfully well."

"Oh, thanks ever so much—— "

"Can we all fit into the back seat? Fine. Hapgood and Hallowes, Studd, please. Yes, the new studio. Long drive, Eddie, I'm afraid."

"Bore if you've got to do it regularly."

"I think we'll all be spending a lot of time there in the next three weeks—— "

"Your attendance will be incessant, Major."

"Why mine, for God's sake?"

"Unsoldierly, that question. Yours not to reason—— "

"Because, Eddie, marketing is the essence of this operation. Commercials are going to be damned expensive to make when the time comes to make them properly, and even more expensive to put on, and we must know that they're going to make sense as part of a marketing scheme—— "

117

"Oh I see. Audiences—— "

"Audiences, coverage, cost per viewer, cost per *suitable* viewer—a press media plan is child's-play compared to this business, and that side of it is your concern."

"Good Go—oh, all right Christopher. Yes, I see. But as to spending three weeks at wherever we're going to—— "

"New Cross."

"God."

"Full of interest, Major."

"Yes, I must say I'm looking forward to seeing a studio working."

"So am I," said Jonathan.

"The copywriters and so on—— "

"All going to come and look. Very necessary. It's all been laid on with Perkins—— "

"Perkins!"

"Perkins is the big power in all this."

"Christ."

"Almost."

"Ah, there, Cornish. Well well, Melot, very nice to see you out here. Ah, Townsend, all well your end? Fine, fine—— "

"Perhaps, gentlemen, you would come this way?"

"Oh, yes, right—— "

"After you, Major."

"—and this is Malise Fergusson, our Production Chief, Gwylim Hughes, our Director, Odo Lamprey and Bill Blade, our Assistant Directors, That's the core of our little team. Quite a team, if we do say so. Quite a machine. Quite a—— "

"Tea, Mr. Perkins?"

"No time. Absolutely not. Unless, gentlemen, you—— "?

"No no—— "

"Well. Forward! This is the Conference Room, Artistes' dressing-rooms in there, my office, my secretary's office—ah there, my dear—gifted girl, that, godsend to me—Production Office, Projection Room, Auditioning Room, Sound, and *through here*—" he paused portentously—"the Studio."

"Ah——"

"Stand back!"

"Shut that door!"

"It's all right——"

"What do you mean, bloody all right——"

"Silence!"

"Bill?"

"Hullo?"

"Not you. Bill props."

"'Ere."

"Ah, at *last*. Where the hell's the commode? The commode for number sixteen?"

"The *wot*?"

"Commode. C-O-M-M-O——"

"Ow! On set."

"On *set*? Ah, I see, yes, so it is. Bill!"

"'Ere."

"Not you. Bill lights."

"'Ere."

"Half, er, and that overhead thing, and this, no, *this*——"

"*Look out*!"

"Eeek!"

"God, near one."

"It's all right, dear, only a bit of wood——"

"Nearly *brained* me——"

"There there——"

"Silence, please, silence, oh I say, can't you stop talking—oh I see, well can't you *whisper* —oh I see, well, we'll just have to wait, then, till you've finished——"

"*Look out!*"

"EEK!"

"Christ."

"Bill."

"'Ere."

"No, Bill *lights* — can't you keep that bloody timber of yours up there? You're pelting it down on to the set like snowflakes, man, nearly wrote off a table—— "

"What about *me*—nearly wrote *me* off—— "

"Plenty of model girls, dear, but tables come expensive—"

"Stand back, vere, please—how can we move vis—— camera wive all you—— s standing abaht like a lot of —— s—— "

"Yes, would you very kindly—— "

"Stan back per*lease*—— "

"*Very* kindly—oh Mr. Perkins, so sorry, didn't see you, was it anything?"

"No no. Just taking a dekko—just taking a peer—just. . . ."

"This is all very interesting."

"Isn't it? The hive, I call it. Hive of activity, *you* know. A hive with no drones, I call it. A hive full only of workers, I call it. A queen, of course, too, ha ha—— "

"You—— ?"

"Well, ha ha—— "

"Are they making a film now, Perkins?"

"Heavens no, they're taking it easy just now. But they're shooting in a few minutes, I fancy—yes, in a hour or two, I fancy. A beauty. Not at liberty to explain it—shouldn't be looking at this, really, but stretch a point, stretch a point—but take it from me, a real beauty, yes."

"Ah—— "

"Stan back, vere, please—— "

"Silence—oh I see—— "

"Look out!"

"*EEEK*!"

"Bill!"

"Darling, how late you are."

"Sorry. I've been spending a fantastic afternoon with Perkins."

"The Television Director."

"Directing away like mad."

"Golly. Where?"

"Their new studio. It's at New Cross."

"Where's that?"

"Half way to Dover."

"*What?*"

"Well, Lewisham. Place was bedlam."

"I bet it was. Interesting?"

"Yes. . . . Yes. The *noise*—— "

"I thought you had to be terribly quiet. I mean, 'silence, roll 'em'—— "

"So did I. Most peculiar."

"It's exhausted you.

"It has rather. Oh—thank you. Sue, you shouldn't—oh darling, thank you. . . ."

"Oh, hullo Eddie. They're all here."

"Morning Lavinia. Am I late?"

"No. They were all frightfully early. Mr. Perkins—— "

"Ah—— "

"Mr. *Fergusson* is that very dark man called? Seems odd—— "

"Yes, doesn't it? Well. I'd better go on in—— "

"Ah, Melot—— "

"Morning, Perkins. Morning, Mr. Fergusson, Mr. er, er—— "

"Lamprey. Odo Lamprey."

"Of *course*. Morning, morning—— "

"The idea this morning, Major, is to finalize some of the treatments our copy people have done. We think a round table meeting may be the best way of doing it—we'll try it, anyway. We specify the advertising requirements, marketing points come from you, design ideas from George here, representing the art side, and our guests can tell us in each case what they can do on film—— "

"And what we *can't* do, Mr. Townsend, remember that—— "

"Ah yes, to be sure. Well, shall we start with the Belgravia Bond script, Uncle Jonathan?"

"As you like, Christopher. It's your meeting."

"Right. Here's the treatment put forward by the copy-writer. We think it's rather a good idea, and I've seen some-thing on the same lines done very effectively on the American television screen. Have a look at it and see what you think."

"Ah. Mm. Mm. No."

"No?"

"Not *filmic*."

"Oh—— "

"Let me put it this way, er—— "

"I think Malise means that the idea is not quite, er—— "

"Perhaps we can explain it this way—— "

"Well suppose, now, for instance, you opened on a tight close-up of a hand writing with a *lovely* quill pen on—— "

"But—— "

" —a big sheet of this paper. Dead silence, d'you see, just the scratch of the quill on the paper—— "

"But it doesn't scratch. At least it's not supposed to. That's the whole basis this brand of paper's sold on— '*Not a scratch in the alphabet*'!"

"Well, then, music—— "

"What about—what about—I've got it! What about a heavenly choir—heavenly C-H-O-I-R, see, tying up with quire, Q-U-I-R-E, a heavenly quire, see?"

"That's *it*, Odo boy, that's *it*—— "

"But—— "

"We've been discussing this one script for two hours, gentlemen—we've got more than fifty more to look at—do you think we might perhaps move on?"

"Well, all right—seems a pity, though, we might solve this one any moment now, really, I feel—— "

"Well, but —— "

"*What* time, darling?"

"Yes, I'm afraid so. I promised Jonathan and Christopher I'd be at the office at eight. We're filming all day—— "

"What fun."

"Well—— "

"Or not?"

"Nothing's decided, that's the trouble. Tomorrow will be chaos. God, I'm tired—oh darling, thank you. . . ."

"This is chaos."

"Yes, they do seem a bit—— "

"A bit disorg—— "

"*Look out!*"

"Bill!"

"Sorry cocky. You all right, dear?"

"No."

"That's O.K. then. Dolly up a bit, Steve, and—— "

"Where d'you want vese?"

"Dolly *up*, you clot, and—— "

"Where d'you want vese?"

"And let's have some more light, yes, that's right, and Bill—— "

"Yes?"

"No, Bill make-up—— "

"Where do you—*want*—*vese?*"

"Touch her up a bit, see, she's melting, see . . what? What are those things?"

"Dunno. Where do you want 'em? For—— 's sake decide cos they're—— ing heavy."

"Oh. Well, let's see—— "

"Ah, Cornish, ah there Townsend, my dear Melot, well met—I haven't, I fear, had as much time as I would have wished to explain to you the way we're tackling your problems—— "

"Oh well—— "

"Silence!"

"Tush."

"Oh, sorry Mr. Perkins."

"Perfectly all right—forgivable, quite forgivable—we won't say another word about it. Well. Let me give you an idea—it'll have to be just an idea, since a full explanation would involve technical language which, *as yet*, you—— "

"Yes yes."

"Well. That group of men over there—all well, you men? Splendid, splendid, that's the ticket—that group who *appear* to be unoccupied are in fact. . . . What? Oh, all right dear. Gentlemen, I'm afraid I must beg you to excuse me for a moment—a call from a prospective client who shall be nameless. . . . Well—I'll tell you this much, he makes soap—but never a word, never a word!"

"Good God."

"All ready? All *really* ready?"

"Yes."

"Yes."

"Lights?"

"Ready."

"Well, at *last*. Got those cues clear?"

"Course!"

"Cameras?"

"Ready."

"You ready, dear ?"

"Er, yes, I think so—— "

"Right. Here we go *at last*, and this time for God's sake. . . . What? Tea break? Oh all right, ten minutes, then. . . . What? Oh all right, twenty minutes then—— "

"Really, Eddie? This evening? Yes, we'd love to, of course."

"Oh good. It's not a party—just you and Clare—— "

"Perfect. We're dying to see your new flat. Seven? Seven-thirty?"

"Seven-thirty, I should think."

"Perfect."

"All right then, *are we all ready*?"

"Yes."

"Yers."

"Bill—*all* of you?"

"All ready."

"Lights? Cameras?"

"Yep."

"You all right dear?"

"Er . . . ooh—— "

"Jesus, the girl's tight."

"Don't know as I blame her—wish I was meself."

"Tight? Don't be soft. She's fainted."

"Why? Answer me that. Fainted indeed."

"No . . . I'm all right . . . It's just standing all this time in all these lights—— "

"You look *terrible* , dear. Ought to go and lie down, I suppose, really. Still, colour won't show on the telly, thank goodness, so we'll go ahead and shoot just the same."

"I'm terribly sorry . . . I just can't—— "

"Nonsense, keep your pecker up, soon be over now—— "

"Not another word, my dear Cornish, not another word. Delighted to see you here. Come again, come again. You see us at our best today, I fancy—the hive has been buzzing—ha ha—has it not? Well well. Now, you must excuse me, I'm afraid—— "

"Ready up there?"

"Yers."

"Ready, dear?"

"Oh . . . again?"

"*Jus'* once or twice more—— "

"All r-right . . . oooh—— "

"Gor, she's gone and fainted again."

"Tight, that's what she is. Wish I was."

"D'you know, Jonathan's given me a car?"

"*Has* he, Clare?"

"Can you drive?"

"No, but he's teaching me. He's having a terrible time."

"On the contrary, darling, you're learning very fast."

"Oh good. . . . I do like this wallpaper, Sue."

"Oh, thank you. We looked at *hundreds*—— "

"Yes, it's so difficult to find one that's nice *and* unusual. Nearly all the nice ones are so ordinary, and nearly all the unusual ones are so awful."

"... *learning very fast*—— "
"*Shut up, Eddie.*"

"Can we all fit in the back seat? Oh good. Yes, Studd, please."
"Is this going to be like Wednesday?"
"Yes, Major, exactly like Wednesday."
"God."

"Can we all fit in? . . . Yes, office, please, Studd."
"Worse than Wednesday."
"Even worse."
"Much worse. Who would have thought it possible?"

"*What*, darling?"
"Yes, the union rules are fantastic. Even that wouldn't have mattered so much if the cameras hadn't broken down."
"All of them?"
"Both of them."
"Oh. . . . You know, you look *too* tired, darling. Are you sure you're all right?"
"Oh yes—yes, I think so. Oh thank you, darling—— "

"Hul*lo*, Eddie, er, hul*lo*—— "
"Hullo Lavinia, it was kind of you to ask us—— "
"No, of *course* not—well, I expect you know every-body—— "
"Of course, his last film was a disaster."
"So was the one before."
"Of course. But in 1924—— "
"Ah well, then the cinema *was* the cinema—— "
"Hullo, Victoria."
"Hul*lo*, er—— "
"Hullo, Angelica."

"Her last book was pathetic—oh, hul*lo*, er—but there was a time when—— "

"Hullo, Clare. Enjoying yourself?"

"Oh, Sue, good. No, not very much."

"Nor are we. Let's go and have some dinner. Where's Jonathan? Oh I see. Well, soon, don't you think?"

"Yes."

"Yes."

"Are we all here? Good. Well, gentlemen—— "

"Just a minute, *just* a minute Mr. Townsend, please. Sorry to interrupt, but I feel— *we* feel—that we really ought to wait for Mr. Perkins."

"Oh—of course, yes. . . . "

"Don't you think, gentlemen, we could go over perhaps just a *few* of these points without Mr. Perkins?"

"No, Mr. Townsend, I'm afraid I don't—*we* don't— really and truly—— "

"Oh, all right."

"God, what a morning."

"Morning? It's three o'clock."

"Oh . . . so it is."

"Let's have a drink."

"Two."

"Millions."

"I say, are you all right, Major?"

"Yes, certainly. Why?"

"Oh, well—you look a bit odd. . . ."

"Who wouldn't, after a morning like that?"

"There's that, to be sure. But—— "

"No, really, I'm fine."

"Oh . . . good."

128

"Next weekend? Are you sure, Jonathan? I mean, so soon before the wedding?"

"Certainly, Eddie. We shall be most disappointed if—— "

"Oh well, thank you very much. I'd better ring Sue up—— "

"Do. And I'm asking you, Eddie, on *condition* that you sit quite still in a deep chair all weekend—— "

"Oh, ha ha, I'm not that tired—— "

"Never mind. That's the condition."

"Oh, ha ha, all right."

"Tickets please."

"Isn't it *cold*?"

"Now now, mother, not that bad."

"Oh it *is*, Henry."

"Seasonable weather, Mr. Tomkins!"

"It is, Mr. Judd, it is."

"Well, well, we mustn't complain, eh?"

"No indeed, no indeed."

"Coming, dear? *Coming, dear*?"

"Tickets, please."

"Henry, I declare I can't find my platform ticket!"

"Well, you'll never find it with your gloves on, Mother."

"But I can't take them off, silly, it's too cold."

"All there except the hatbox."

"Hatbox? *Hat*box?"

"You know, Ralph. Round thing with a hat inside."

"Oh very good, dear, very good indeed—— "

"Tickets, please."

"All right, young man, all right—oh, it's Mr. Tomkins, good evening Mr. Tomkins, isn't it cold? Well, as I was saying to Henry here—drat the boy, where's he gone? Oh yes, yoo-hoo, Henry, it's all right, dear, it's only Mr. Tomkins, he won't mind."

"Now, mother, really—— "

"Brrr."

"There they are! Good evening, er—— "

"Good evening, sir. Good evening, Mrs. Melot, m'm."

"Good evening, Hullo, Daphne, so you've come to meet us again, how *very* nice. . . . Hullo, Jeremy."

"Hullo Daphne. Hullo Jeremy. Has, er, Miss Perkins come yet?"

"Ha ha. He means Auntie Clare."

"Yeth, ha ha."

"Auntie Clare, I mean."

"She's wizard, Auntie Clare."

"Thuper."

"Yes, she is, isn't she? Has she come?"

"Of course not. We shouldn't have come to meet you if *she'd* been at home."

"No, quite right, jolly sensible—— "

"Oh dear, here you are—I mean, how very nice that you were able to come—— "

"It's very nice to be here, Mrs. Connell."

"But so bitterly cold—— "

"Not in here."

"Oh, I am so thankful you say so. I was quite worried you might find it—— "

"Find it . . .?"

"Oh—— "

"The children seem very well."

"Yes *indeed*—— "

"And so much looking forward to Clare's visit."

"Yes *indeed*, as am I. Dear Clare, I do hope my brother Jonathan remembers to have a good thick rug in the car—— "

"It's a very warm car."

"Oh, *do* you find it so?"

"Yes, don't you?"

"Yes . . . yes, I do——"

"Clare, dear, you're looking lovely."

"Thank you, Sue. I feel all—all glowy."

"I don't wonder. Oh—here's Christopher. Hullo, Christopher."

"Hullo, Sue. Didn't expect me, eh? Hullo, you horrid old Major."

"Are we going to have any conferences, Christopher?"

"We should."

"Yes, we should."

"But I don't think we will, do you?"

"No, I don't think we will."

"Certainly not. I forbid it."

"Oh, hullo, Jonathan. Good drive?"

"Perfect, thank you Eddie. Bit of snow—rather a bore—but. . . ."

"Snow—oh God——"

"Major——"

"Shut up, Christopher. I reserve the right——"

"—yes, I agree, Eddie darling, Clare and I both think you ought to go to bed."

"What, now? What about my din-din?"

"Din-din in bed."

"Oh no——"

"Oh yes."

"Yes, Eddie, do really. You're not looking——"

"Oh . . . all right. Thank you."

"What a day, darling."

"Heaven."

"Look at those trees."

"Absolute heaven."

"I love this crunchy feeling on the grass."

"So do I, except my toes are getting cold."

"Nobody *knows*—— "

"Tiddely pom—— "

"That's enough."

"Quite enough. Where are all the others?"

"*Well*. Mrs. C. and the children have gone into Basingstoke. So has Jonathan, come to think of it."

"Clare too?"

"No, she's somewhere around."

"Christopher is who I really want, actually."

"Darling, you're not going to have a television conference on a morning like this?"

"Well—— "

"Listen, (*a*) you mustn't because of the morning, (*b*) you mustn't because I won't allow it, (*c*) Christopher's disappeared, and (*d*)—— "

"All right, darling, (*c*)'s convinced me."

"Woof, I feel full."

"So do I. Let's go in the library, Christopher."

"All right. Well, here are all the scripts—let's start with this goddam Belgravia thing."

"Right. Where were you all morning?"

"Why? Was anyone looking for me?"

"No, not that I know of."

"Good. Now, concentrate, Major. Belgravia."

"Er, yes. . . . You know, something's wrong with the costing on this."

"Something's wrong with everything about it. Let's see—— "

"Good morning, gentlemen, good morning good morning. Good to see you out here again—— "

"Morning, Perkins. We've got all these scripts for you, a good deal revised—— "

"Ah ha! Revisions, eh? We too, in our little way, would like to suggest some minor modifications—some minor adjustments—some minor. . . ."

"Yes, er—— "

"Silence! Oh, sorry . . . Er, Bill—— "

"Look out!"

"Shall we sit here?"

"Oh—all right, if this is really—— "

"Certainly, my dear fellow, certainly."

"Can't sit there, Mr. Perkins sir, sorry, we're just—— "

"Ah yes, to be sure, well—— "

"Look out!"

"Or there, Mr. Perkins, if I was you."

"Ah yes—— "

"Know something? That fellow's going to faint same as that girl did las' week."

"Tight. Tell it a mile off. Lucky bastard."

"Are you feeling all right, Major ?"

"Yes, thanks—— "

"A specific! You require a specific! May I suggest—— "

"No no, Perkins, thanks—— "

"Tight. Wish I was."

"Yes, Studd, please. D'you know, I don't believe I can stand another day like that?"

"Nor I."

"No, you don't look as if you could, Eddie, I must say—— "

"Oh, Mr. Melot—— "

"Well, Jacqueline?"

"Er—you don't look too grand, you know, really you don't. Oughtn't you to—well, I do hope I'm not speaking out of turn, Mr. Melot, but—— "

"That's all right, Jacqueline—but I'm fine, thank you."

"Oh *good*. Er. . . ."

"You're wearing a new dress, aren't you, Jacqueline? *Very* smart."

"Ooh—do you think so? I made it myself, you know."

"Well, that's wonderful, Jacqueline, simply wonder-full—— "

"I say, careful—speak of the devil. . . . Morning, Cornish."

"Morning, Jervis. Coming, Eddie?"

"Yes, shan't be a second, just got to wash—— "

"All right. I'll be upstairs."

"—yes, gone. Yes, I quite agree, most astonishing. Charming girl, absolutely charming. I think he might have fared a lot further and—— "

"Yes, I suppose so. Sweet girl, yes. But, dammit, the ages—— "

"Oh I know, quite a difference, but after all—— "

"*Is* Mr. Perkins coming?"

"Oh yes, Mr. Townsend, most certainly he is. Isn't he, Odo?"

"Oh yes indeed."

"Oh . . . well, I suppose we'd better wait—— "

"I do think so, really, Mr. Townsend."

"I'll be in my office, Christopher, if you gentlemen will excuse me?"

"Of course, Mr. Melot, yes of course—— "

"O.K. Major. I'll ring you."

"Oh dear, what a lot of people—— "

"Where's Jonathan? Oh, there he is——"

"Oh, *good*, here you are, come in Sue, Eddie——"

"Hullo, Jonathan—— ooh, how delicious, thank you. . . . Hullo, Clare."

"Hullo, Sue—hullo, Eddie—I am glad you could come."

"Yes, well, it's all right once one gets inside—oh, thank you, Jonathan, marvellous. . . . What a lot of people? Are we frightfully late?"

"Dreadfully."

"Oh dear——"

"You've met my father, Sue, haven't you?"

"Oh yes—good evening, Mr. Perkins."

"Good evening. Miss er——"

"Mrs., Father. Mrs. Melot."

"Oh yes, I'm sorry, Mrs.——"

"There's Lavinia, hullo Lavinia——"

"Hul*lo*, er——"

"I remember you, do I not, Mr. er——"

"*Melot.*"

"Melot. Did you not come to my house for tea one evening?"

"Yes indeed, a most enjoyable party——"

"Did you find it so? I can't say the same, I fear. Mrs. Perkins's cousins from Highbury are so very—what shall I say?—censorious. They contribute very little to the, er, party spirit——"

"Yes, I remember that they were rather silent——"

"They had some inexplicable prejudice—*have*, I regret to say, some inexplicable prejudice—against my prospective son-in-law, with whom, I believe, you work?"

"Yes. Yes, I do."

"Quite. I have told Mrs. Perkins's cousins that to be an enemy of the system—as, I may say, I myself am—it is not necessary to be an enemy of the individual."

"No, no—— "

"And particularly when that individual is not only about to become, so to say, a member of the family, but is also so intelligent and courteous a person as Jonathan—— "

"Yes—— "

"Forgive me asking, but are you feeling quite well, Mr. er—— ? "

"Melot."

"Mr. *Melot*. Because you look—— "

"No, I'm quite all right, thank you—— "

"Eddie, I say Eddie, stand up—— "

"Is he stinking?"

"So soon? Surely not."

"No, I'm fine—— "

"I don't believe you are, you know—— "

"Really I am."

"Darling, don't you think—— ?"

"No, honestly—— "

"Oh . . . all right. But—— "

"Ah there, Melot, well met, well met—— "

"Oh, hullo—— "

"Feeling dicky? A specific—you shall have a specific—— "

"Oh, Adrian, please—— "

"Ah there, Sis, I was telling our friend—— "

"Would you like to lie down for a bit, Eddie?"

"No no—— "

"Whoops—steady The Buffs—— "

"Adrian!"

"I say, careful—— "

"I do believe he's passed out."

"Have you hit your head?"

"Darling!"

"It—it's all right—— "

"I don't believe it is, you know."

"Is he stinking?"

"No no, surely not. Ill, more."

"Ah. Then shouldn't we loosen his collar—ah, you have. . . ."

"Air! Give him air!"

"No, I'm all right—— "

"Can you manage, Christopher?"

"Yes, yes. Come on Sue, we'll get him into the car—— "

"Oh Christopher, thank you. Darling, how do you feel?" But I couldn't answer.

PART THREE

Summer in Cornwall

Chapter One

✣

It was midsummer before I was really well. When the worst of my illness was over, Sue and I went abroad, as much to rest her as to complete my cure; we got back to England late in May and started living normally again. We were both enormously well and very happy. Though we had had a wonderful, tranquil time at a farm in the hills behind Grasse, I was glad to get back to my job and Sue was glad to get back to our flat and to the business of getting ready for the baby which, to our delight, we now knew she was expecting.

I vividly remember driving to the office on the Monday morning after we got back. Hyde Park was full of people—men in shirt-sleeves, boys playing cricket, girls in cotton dresses: I wondered how they all managed to be so unoccupied, but I was glad they all were because they made the park populous and gay, suiting my mood.

I reached the office at about ten. I was touched at the pleasure the little receptionist showed when she saw me, and I walked to my room with a springy step.

Jacqueline was waiting for me.

"Oh Mr. *Melot*, how wonderful to see you back!"

"Hullo, Jacqueline. Er, thank you. It's very nice to be back."

"We've missed you dreadfully."

"Oh, really?—— "

"The department just hasn't seemed the same—— "

"Well, I expect you all got on very well without me."

"Oh, how *can* you say that, Mr. Melot? We've been struggling, simply struggling—— "

"It's nice to think so, but I expect really you all managed far better for my being away—— "

"How *can* you say that?"

"Ha ha, well, er, you're very smart, Jacqueline."

"I put on my best dress to welcome you."

"How very nice of you," I said, touched. "And some flowers! How very kind!"

"Aren't they lovely? They're from Mrs. Cornish."

"Really? I do think that's kind of her. I must ring her up and thank her—— "

"And, Mr. Melot, the Chairman said could you go and see him, if it was convenient, when you arrived."

"Aha, I'll go and see him at once, then."

My reunion with Lavinia was all that I had feared; my reunion with Jonathan was all that I had hoped. He made me feel that it was only by the most outrageous luck, only by a series of desperate contrivances and accidents, that the firm had succeeded in surviving the disaster of my absence; he made me feel that my return was the most fortunate thing that had happened to him professionally for years; he made me feel, as he doubtless intended, very glad indeed to be back.

Then he began to talk about television.

"You know all that ridiculous work we did last winter with Hapgood and Hallowes?"

"The Perkins episode? Do I not?"

"Yes. I shall always believe that the New Cross studio was responsible for your illness, Eddie."

"I don't doubt it helped."

"Yes. We knew we were paying a lot for those films, but who would have thought the price was going to be *that* high? Anyway, you've come back at an interesting moment, because after a thousand delays and breakdowns of every sort we are at last about to see the whole lot finished."

"Good God—haven't you seen them yet?"

"No. Fantastic, isn't it? We've made a great deal of fuss, as you may imagine, but my brother-in-law—— "

"Your brother-in-law?"

"Adrian Perkins."

"Oh—of course."

"He and Sir Hilary between them have held out against even Christopher's most strenuous attempts to look at the things any sooner. Sir Hilary, by the way—a most extra-ordinary thing—you won't recognize him. He's absolutely transformed."

"What into?"

"Well, a sort of gentle background figure who never gives anyone any trouble at all."

"*What?*"

"Yes, I couldn't believe it at first, when I saw him recently. Hadn't seen him for some time. Came as rather a shock. Christopher tells me it's been a steady process for months."

"Has he been ill?"

"No, and it's not senility either—he's not much older than I am. I don't believe it's even the strain of a new medium, because from all I gather he doesn't take any strain. My brother-in-law takes it all. That's the oddest part about it. What Sir Hilary's really become, Christopher says, is a kind of super yes-man to my brother-in-law."

"Good God."

"You may well say so, Eddie, you may well say so. Well, coming back to these films we're supposed to be seeing today—— "

"Oh, it's actually today?"

"Yes, didn't I tell you? This very morning. They wouldn't let us so much as peep till now—said they wouldn't let us run the risk of being prejudiced by seeing anything short of what they consider an adequate standard. Said it would be unfair to us and to them."

"I see their point in a way."

"So did I, Eddie, so did I, four months ago."

"There's that, of course."

"There is. Still, today's the day. I'm all excited, I must say. We've got to go to some odd little cinema in Soho, at eleven o'clock. Would you like to come? Or would you rather look at your own people and get settled down first?"

"No—I can get settled down later. I'd love to see the films."

"Good. We ought to go soon, actually—I'll whistle up Christopher. . . . Oh, here he is. Morning, Christopher——"

"Morning, Uncle Jonathan. . . . Major! They told me you were coming back today, but I didn't dare bank on it. How splendid to see you! You look very well—are you?"

"Yes, very, thanks."

"Oh *good*. So you ought to be by now. How's Sue?"

"Full of beans."

"Good. She looked pretty exhausted when you left."

"She was, I'm afraid. But we had a terrifically placid time—did absolutely nothing for weeks. She's fine now."

"I am glad. And I'm most excited by your news—your last letter, I think——"

"Our family, as they say—yes, we're very pleased. . . ."

"Of course you are. So am I. I can't think of any race I would rather see procreated than yours, you ludicrous old Major. I shall expect to be asked to the christening."

"You shall be. Your present will have to be very expensive, to mark your devoted appreciation of the qualities of character you have always so much admired in the child's father."

"Prodigal, I shall be. Rashly extravagant. Seven-and-six, at least—— "

"Come on," said Jonathan, "we ought to go."

"All right. Coming, Major? You must."

"Of course I am. I wouldn't miss this for anything."

"Well, you *may* be right. After months of struggling to achieve this consummation, I'm not sure I quite have the courage to face it."

"Oh Christopher," said Jonathan, "some of them will be bad, no doubt, but some of them—— "

"Will be worse."

"Well, they're only experiments."

"Vivisection," said Christopher gloomily. "Doctor used his Instrument. I tell you I'm dreading this show. Thank God it's good and private."

"Yes, I must admit I agree there."

We were greeted by Perkins, very point-device, and Sir Hilary, as mutely and astonishingly deferential as I had been warned to expect, but still wearing his aggressive tweeds. The cinema, when we filed in, seemed completely full. We were told that the rows of small, grey-faced men were all H. & H. technicians whose presence was indispensable—"to explain."

"To explain what?" asked Christopher.

"Technicalities."

"But—— "

"To laymen such as yourselves," said Perkins firmly, "many of these films may seem—how shall I put it?—— "

"Bad?"

"No no. Indeed not. Good. But there will be details— there will be specific, I might say particular, points—er, which, *as* laymen, may perhaps surprise you—which will perhaps confuse you. Experts such as all of my good colleagues here will be able to make clear to you why we have, in certain cases, done as we have done. Eh, Hilary?"

"That's right, Adrian. Er, yes, indeed."

"Ah," said Jonathan, "yes."

"But," said Christopher, "is the public going to get the same sort of explanations from your experts? I mean, when the housewife gets all puzzled and confused— "

"Now there, my dear Townsend, you touch on my favourite hobby-horse. Let me expound to you my—I should say *our*—philosophy of visual selling in the context of the contemporary climate of—Mm?" He was interrupted by plucking at his sleeve. "What?"

"Ready, Mr. Perkins."

"Ah good. A moment, please, while I tell our friends about our credo of visual selling— "

"Perhaps later," said Jonathan.

"We might look at these films first," said Christopher.

"Or you could write it all down for us," I suggested.

"No no. I would rather you saw these films in the context of a full knowledge of the creative convictions which inspired their, er, creation, Don't you agree, Hilary?"

"Yes of course," said Sir Hilary, "yes indeed."

"We've only got the theatre for an hour, Mr. Perkins," said a little man with a single etiolated lock of hair wandering across a bare, narrow skull. "It's been booked by someone else at twelve-thirty."

"Ah there, Cavendish. Do you know Cavendish, gentlemen? My right hand man. I often wonder where I should be without him, eh, Cavendish?"

"Oh Mr. Perkins— "

"I mean it, I really do. My right hand man."

"Oh Mr. Perkins. Still, there it is, if we're to get through the programme by twelve-thirty, we'll have to start now, you know."

"Very well, very well." Perkins turned to us, deprecatingly. "We are the slaves of time, are we not? Never mind. Not another word. Sit down, gentlemen, make yourselves at home. All set? Comfortable? Comfortable, Melot? Splendid, splendid. All well, you men? Good. Then let the show commence!"

The lights dimmed and went off and we all sat expectantly in the dark. After a long pause, violent images of dazzling brilliance began to erupt on the screen: upside-down figures of huge size flashed up in succession, to be succeeded by explosive white shapes. The silence remained absolute. Presently the screen went black again, and then, amid an almost palpable exhalation of relief from the dark rows of experts, a recognizable picture appeared: the giant figure of Perkins, dramatically lit from below, standing like a piece of Aztec sculpture before a background of winking stars and criss-crossing searchlights. Unseen trumpets sounded a fanfare. Then the hieratic figure began to speak:

"Ladies and gentlemen, my name is Adrian Porter-Perkins. It is my privilege and pleasure to introduce to you a series of brief films created by myself and my gifted colleagues of Hapgood and Hallowes Limited as a major step towards the realization on the television screens of the millions of British viewers of tomorrow of the highest principles of contemporary creative advertising. The films you are about to see were made at our New Cross studios; they represent, we firmly believe, an important contribution to the history of the visual techniques of publicity; they will give you, we are proudly confident, the strongest reasons for consulting us with all your film and television problems. Ladies and gentlemen—" the huge face swam forward into tight close-up "—a programme of experimental advertising films from Hapgood and Hallowes, Showmen Extra-ordinary!"

The trumpets gave another, longer, fanfare. Perkins's face dissolved amid the stars and searchlights. There was an extended moment of black silence. Then a baffling image came gradually into near-focus: areas of white, arbitrarily spread across a variously-toned dark background. The scene swam away from one's eyes and revealed itself, presently, as a badly photographed, very close close-up of a hand writing a letter at a desk. There was still complete silence. After a moment the watcher became further with-drawn from the scene, and one was able to take in the owner of the hand (and presumably the desk): an infinitely distinguished gentleman with silver hair, wearing a white tie and a great many medals. His mouth began to open and close. He indicated, with grave appreciation, the sheets of writing-paper in front of him. He picked up, finally, the box from which he had evidently taken this paper, and held it towards us so that we were able to read, as after too many glasses darkly, the words "Belgravia Bond" dimly in-scribed across it.

After the first few seconds of this elegant dumb-show a restive movement was perceptible among the experts.

"No sound."

"What's happened to the sound?"

"There ought to be sound with this one."

"Something's gone wrong with the sound."

"The sound," cried Perkins, "what of the sound?"

"There doesn't seem to be any, Mr. Perkins."

"Nor there does," said Christopher.

"Patience, my dear Townsend, patience I beseech you—— "

"Er, Mr. Perkins," said Cavendish, "shall I go and see what's happened to the sound?"

"*Do*, my dear fellow, *do*."

"Oke. Coming, Vernon?"

"I better, I think, don't you?"

"Yes, you better, I think. All right, Mr. Perkins?"

"Yes, carry on, men. Discover the cause of the failure. Put matters to rights. Lose no time, not a second. Leave no stone unturned." He turned to us. "Well, gentlemen, this little *contretemps* will doubtless be overcome in a twinkling — will certainly be put right in a second — "

"Oh good."

"Meanwhile it gives us a chance to discuss the opening. Do you like the opening?"

"Er— "

"Well— "

"Let me explain to you why we determined on so directly *personal* an approach to the problem of introducing our series. We decided, after, I assure you, the most exhaustive and careful thought — we felt, and I think I speak for all of us when I say this, that— "

A crash interrupted him. Then the violent fantasies that had preceded Perkins's appearance on the screen were repeated; so presently, was Perkins himself against his cosmic background. This time, however, Perkins's mouth opened and closed, as had that of his elderly letter-writer, quite soundlessly.

"Oh tush," said Perkins (our flesh and blood Perkins), "what can have happened now?"

"I don't know, Mr. Perkins."

"Nor do I, Mr. Perkins, I'm sure."

"I think something's wrong."

"I think it must be."

"Have a dekko, some of you men, will you? Never mind," he turned to us again, "never mind. Let me pick up where I left off. Er— "

But again a crash interrupted him; again came the vivid

surrealism of the upside-down numbers and the white ex-
plosions. The trumpet fanfare this time sounded as it should:
but before the giant Perkins could begin his speech he disappeared in a brilliant flash and was succeeded by silent
blackness.

"Film's broke," said a heavy voice.

"Daresay it has."

"Looks like it, anyway."

"It *does* look like it."

"I think," said Christopher, "that the film has broken."

"Impossible," said Perkins uneasily.

"The film's broke, Mr. Perkins," said an expert. "But
we'll fix it, shall we?"

"*Do*, my dear fellow."

"Yuss, we'll fix it. Come on, Vernon."

"Broke good and proper."

"Looks like it."

The morning wore on.

By half past twelve we had seen the upside-down figures
and the Perkins and the searchlights many times, variously
with and without accompanying sound. We had also been
vouchsafed glimpses of the letter-writing scene, without
sound, and (by accident) a few seconds of what looked like
the last act of *Giselle* executed backwards. Through it all ran
the funeral chorus of the experts and the gay obbligato of
Perkins. At half past twelve we were still ready to enjoy
whatever other combinations of these elements the pro-
jectionist could extract from his roll of film, when a little
fussy man with a resplendent tie told Perkins that our time
was up.

"Time *up*?" cried Perkins. "*Up*?"

"Yes, sir, up it is. Half twelve, that's the time by my
watch and chain, and that's your time up, sir, I'm sorry to say."

"Well well, I think I must ask you to extend our time a little—— "

"Can't be done, sir, quite out of the question—— "

"Make it worth your while, I need hardly say—— "

"No sir, quite impossible I'm afraid. I have clients waiting, other clients, sir, waiting—— "

"My company is not without resources to make it *well* worth your while, eh, Hilary?"

"Er, yes. Yes."

"No sir, simply not possible, I'm afraid, not on the cards at all. I must really ask you to clear the theatre, if you'll be so very good, and let my clients, my other clients, in—— "

"Rather a farce, that."

"Rather a farce, Uncle Jonathan, yes. I'm sorry."

"Not your fault, Christopher."

"No. I wonder whose?"

"Er—— "

"I'd better try and find out."

"Yes, will you?"

"Oh, by the way, Eddie," said Jonathan a little later, "I knew there was something I had to tell you. A message from Clare, really."

"Clare? How is she?"

"Very well, thank you."

"She very kindly sent me some flowers this morning."

"Did she? I'd no idea."

"I was very pleased. I must thank her."

"Well, come and thank her this evening. Bring Sue."

"Oh—all right. Thank you. Is that the message?"

"That's part of it. The other part is, would you and Sue like to come to the Magdalen commem ball with us the week after next?"

"The Magdalen commem. . . . What an attractive idea."

"Yes, isn't it? I haven't been to one for—oh—twenty years. You haven't, I don't imagine, for—what?"

"Five years."

"Yes. Clare's never been to one."

"Nor has Sue, I'm sure."

"Well, there you are. Four strong reasons why we should all go. Magdalen ones only happen once every three years, and in my day they were supposed to be particularly good."

"And in mine."

"Yes. Christopher reports the same."

"Is he coming?"

"Yes indeed. I forget with whom. Some girl."

"Oh good."

"So we'll count you in, shall we? I am glad, what fun. I'll tell you what we've planned. It's on a Friday, so we thought we'd drive down—or up, I suppose one ought to say—the same afternoon, and change in Oxford somewhere. We'll dine I expect in Woodstock at that very good pub whose name I've forgotten, and then turn up at Magdalen at eleven or whatever time one's supposed to. Then we'll drive back to Fordings when it's all over and stay there recovering for the rest of the weekend. How does that strike you?"

"Magnificent, Jonathan, a magnificent idea. We'd love to come, of course."

"Oh good, Clare will be pleased."

"I wonder if I've still got a white tie?"

"Christopher will lend you one, I don't doubt."

"That's true. We'll go in a punt—— "

"We'll eat strawberries as the sun comes up—— "

"*What* a splendid idea!"

"Yes, isn't it? I feel all excited."

"The last time you felt all excited," I said, "was this morning, just before we saw all those films."

"Yes, I did, didn't I? Is that an omen?"

I laughed. "No no."

"No," he agreed.

Chapter Two

✣

The next fortnight passed quickly and gaily. I had a happy time settling back into the far from uninteresting routine of my job. Jacqueline was all sympathy, all untiring devotion, and far less irritating than I had remembered. My other assistants—nice people who do not come into this story—seemed glad to have me back. Sue was—I can think of no other word—radiant. Christopher was abstracted, but only (I thought) by the ludicrous cares of his special responsibilities. Jonathan was as serenely competent and unfailingly charming as ever, and looking forward with attractively childlike gusto to fun and games in Oxford. And Clare, whom I saw once or twice, did him in all superficial ways more than adequate justice. Sue told me she was very well-dressed and very beautiful: if my own enthusiasm was moderate to the point of being less enthusiasm than relief, I recognized that Sue was probably right. At any rate she seemed as devoted to Jonathan as he to her, and certainly fulfilled all the social duties of her station perfectly.

On the Friday afternoon of the dance we drove to Oxford in three cars. Jonathan and Ciare went in his beautiful black Mercedes. Sue and I went in my Hillman. Christopher and a pleasant, dark girl called Mary Massingham went in his Austin-Healey. It was a magnificent afternoon: high summer had never, to me, looked higher. The green of the heavy beeches by Wycombe, the green of the thick meadows of the river valley, had almost completed their seasonal change from the infinite variation of spring to the rich uniformity of mid-summer. There were certainly flowers; I expect there were birds; the sun was blazing.

We got to Oxford in time for tea, which we all had to-gether in an hotel. We were joined by the ostensible reason for the party, a nice young cousin of Jonathan's, up at Magdalen, called Nigel; he brought a nice little deb called Sarah and another young couple called Tim and Caroline. They made up the rest of our party, which therefore by this time numbered ten.

Tea, as this number suggests, was confused. We sat on chairs a little too deep for comfort before tables a little too low for convenience; we ate toast and sandy yellow cake in a bedlam of foregatherings.

"Oh *there* you are," people kept crying near us.

"Yes, *here* I am," others would reply.

The two undergraduates, as is the way of undergraduates, kept their eyes roving: they constantly greeted remote, un-varying friends, and often stood awkwardly among the cups to be introduced to the remote, unvarying partners of these friends. Everybody, it was clear, was going to the Magdalen commem. I was glad they were. We were all, in the lounge of that hotel, full of happy anticipation.

When we had pushed back our plates and lit cigarettes someone suggested a punt.

"*Yes*," cried Clare, "please."

"Me too," said Sue.

"We must all go," said Christopher, "at once."

We walked to Magdalen and down the steep ramp to the punt-landing under the city side of the bridge; but there was only one punt available.

"We'll squeeze in."

"Ten of us? You're mad."

"Count us out," said Jonathan's young cousin; "we're supposed to be going to a cocktail party in a few minutes anyway."

"That seems a shame, Nigel," said Clare.

"No no, that's all right."

"Count us out, too," said the other undergraduate. "We really ought to show up at the same party."

"Well, if you're sure, Tim—— ."

"Yes yes, we'll see you later."

"That still leaves six of us," said Sue dubiously. "Can we get six of us in a punt?"

"Yes," said Christopher, "six? Certainly."

"We'll sink," said Jonathan.

"No no."

"Yes yes."

"Yes," admitted Christopher. "A thought above the Plimsoll line, I daresay."

"So leave me out too," said Jonathan. "I want to go and look at the Parks."

"Why, darling?"

"There's a cricket match going on. It's the most perfect place in the world to watch a cricket match, and this is the most perfect afternoon to watch a cricket match. I'd far rather, honestly."

"Do you know," said Clare, "I believe he means it."

"Certainly I mean it."

"I'll come too," said Mary Massingham. "I'd really just as soon. I only came down from Cambridge last year and I've had all the punting I need for a bit. I'd love to watch the cricket match."

"Good girl," said Jonathan. "Spoken like a man."

"But that seems too bad," said Clare.

"No honestly."

"Oh, well then, if you're sure— "

"Don't be so seduced by the beauties of nature," said Jonathan, "that you make yourselves late."

"No no, we'll watch the time."

"Good. We'll be seeing you then."

"Good-bye darling, have a nice cricket match."

"Good-bye," said Jonathan tenderly. "Don't drown."

He gave his arm to Mary with an old-world elegance he only partly parodied, and they disappeared up the grey stone ramp.

Christopher stepped into our punt first, took the pole, and stood ready in the stern. It seemed idle to resist so determined a move, so I thankfully settled myself into the cushions of the bow seat. Sue came and stretched out beside me. Clare, clutching her broad black straw hat by its tiny crown, sat gingerly on the shiny imitation leather of the other seat: and we were off. Christopher propelled us expertly round the tricky first corner by the bridge, then up the still, broad backwater by Addison's Walk. Presently, dropping the end of the pole neatly under the edge of the punt, he gave a last enormous push; then he stood still, the pole and his hands dripping. We swam with beautiful precision up the exact middle of the stream for a long, silent moment. When we had nearly stopped Christopher handed Clare the pole.

"Hold this a second, Clare, will you?"

"Eek—it's wet."

"Sorry. This bit's dry."

"Oh—yes. Thank you."

Relieved of the unwieldy pole, Christopher took off his light tweed coat.

"Catch," he said.

"Oof," said Sue, as it landed in her lap. "I'll fold it up for you, Christopher, shall I?"

"Thanks. Don't let my money fall out."

But as he spoke pennies crashed among the duckboards under our feet.

"Ah! There you go, wasting my tiny substance."

"Only pennies, Christopher. You can spare a few pennies."

"That's absolutely true. Today I can. Other days, no. In fact, if I had any more pennies I'd throw them in this wonderful river."

"But you have some more," said Clare, taking the coat and shaking it. "I'll throw them in for you, shall I?"

"Certainly not. On no account. Vicarious largesse—that's a terrible thought. A bad precedent. And what's more—— "

But Clare had already taken a threepenny bit out of his pocket and was holding it over the water.

"No!" said Christopher. "That's threepence!"

"It's an offering," said Sue. "Go on, Clare."

"I forbid it," said Christopher.

"Don't be mean, Christopher. Why are you so mean? We owe it to the river."

"Am I to pay our joint debts?"

"I think he should, don't you?"

"I think he should."

Clare gravely opened her fingers and the small fat coin dropped with an enormous little splash into the river. Before the splash had fully settled back on itself, Christopher lunged down to catch the disappearing threepenny bit: he crashed forward with a strangled shout and plunged his bare arm into the water.

"No good," he said, recovering himself. "Gone."

"All in a good cause," said Clare.

"Oh you minx," said Christopher, shaking his dripping hands at her.

"Christopher, *don't*. . . . You've soaked me."

"You've robbed me."

"Don't——"

Clare collapsed with laughter among the cushions, dropping the pole with a clatter. It teetered, rolled, and splashed over the side of the punt. Perilously leaning out, I grabbed it and hauled it cautiously towards me.

"Thank you, Major," said Christopher. Solemnly he retrieved the pole and lifted it out. Solemnly he stood up and began punting again.

Clare looked round and up at him. "You beast," she said, "Thief."

"Bully."

"Woman," he said with scorn, "woman."

They both laughed quietly, and we shot the wooden bridge that crosses over from Addison's Walk, into the Magdalen Fellows' Garden. As we swung right-handed into the reedy stretch by the water-meadow I decided it was time I punted.

"Christopher," I said, "I will now punt"

"You, Major? Nonsense."

"Yes, I insist."

"He insists," said Sue.

"Rash fool," said Christopher. "Madcap."

"I'm very good at punting," I said. "Besides, you need a rest."

"That's perfectly true, I do."

"Of course you do," said Clare. "You aren't as strong as you were."

"Not nearly," he sighed. "Weaker and poorer."

I took my coat off and left it beside Sue, and Christopher stepped with elaborately pantomimed difficulty over the back of Clare's seat into the middle of the punt. As I moved to take his place he clasped me by the shoulders with a shrill cry of fear. We staggered this way and that, rocking the punt sharply; Clare screamed; Sue giggled. Presently I extricated myself and clambered over to the stern, and Christopher settled down beside Clare. I took the pole, feeling very strong and sun-warmed, and started punting.

I sent the punt slowly up beside the meadow's edge. Other punts were staked to the bank with their own poles, the people in them talking drowsily or lying motionless; couples walked slowly along the path; two men in tennis-clothes, swinging their racquets, cantered past; a small dark bird shot away from the reeds with a loud, silly call and splashed down a few yards off.

We were silent.

Sue was lying back on her cushions. Her red cotton skirt was spread wide on the leather and wood; her tousled fair hair rested on her clasped hands; she was looking up at the clear sky; a leg was drawn up under her in one of those extreme positions which men find so impossible and women so natural. Christopher and Clare, side by side with their backs to me, lolled in attitudes as relaxed and as graceful. Clare, like Sue, stared upwards. By now the sun was low over the woods to our left, and, as we swam through the shadows cast by the small willows on the bank, Clare's vivid upturned face showed alternately golden and white: lit and shaded: strongly angular and smoothly round. Christopher was lower in the seat: his head was level with Clare's shoulder. I could not see in what direction he was looking—in fact I had the feeling, I don't know why, that his eyes were shut.

It was still very warm. The air was absolutely motionless. It was a drugged evening, a hypnotized evening. The swarms of small riverside insects which darted in and out of the low, gold sunlight seemed to swing through a thicker element than air: to gyrate on more languorous wings, and to a remoter purpose, than the insects of an ordinary evening. On the brown water, smooth until we folded it to corduroy, floated a few large leaves. High in one tree a bird rustled.

Low in another hung a huge cobweb. Clare's hand, I noticed, was touching Christopher's.

We whispered past a tethered punt. In it, a girl in yellow shorts was playing a recorder to a girl in blue shorts; the thin, woody notes were breathy and ill-articulated, but they came full and sweet over the water. The tune was "Greensleeves". The magic was curious and I suppose spurious, but it was magic. Sue lifted her head to look, then dropped it back slowly to stare at the sky again. I lifted the punt-pole clear of the water and held it still: it dripped little silver streams into our dark wake. Clare's head shifted a little to the right and down: towards Christopher. Christopher's head shifted a little to the left and up: towards Clare. I think they looked at each other. The punt was hardly moving. The world was hardly moving.

"I always think that's such a nice piece," said the girl in the yellow shorts, taking the recorder from her lips. She spoke in a flat Midland accent.

"What a pity," murmured Sue.

Clare and Christopher both settled back. The moment passed. But I was sure that something very important had happened.

What had happened?

Clare and Christopher had exchanged a glance. Sitting side by side in a wide punt, hardly touching, in broad daylight, and in the presence of a married couple, they had exchanged a glance because a female undergraduate from Somerville or St. Hugh's had been playing a well-known air inexpertly on a recorder.

But what had happened?

At half past seven Sue and I were dressing in an hotel bedroom. I was shaving. Sue, in her blue cotton dressing-gown, was doing her nails.

"Sue—— "

"Yes?"

"That girl playing the recorder in that punt—— "

"Yes, wasn't that odd? It made me feel—I don't know—very old."

"What do you mean, darling?"

"Or very young."

"It seemed to be affecting the others, too."

"Did it?"

"Yes, didn't you notice?"

"Notice what?"

"Christopher and Clare," I said. "Christopher and Clare."

"What was there to notice? Was there anything to notice?"

"Well—no. Not really. But I noticed it just the same."

"I can't think what you're talking about, darling."

"No, I quite agree. But I'm worried."

"Well, don't be."

"I can't help it. There's something wrong going on."

"You're dotty. What could there be? For one thing, would you say Christopher was *at all* that sort of person?"

"Well, no. . . ."

"No. And for another, would you say Clare was likely to risk everything she's got—— "

"No. . . ."

"No. You've been ill, darling," she smiled at me gently, "and I'm taunting you with your weakness."

"Bitch."

Holding her hands stiffly behind her so as not to smudge the wet nail-varnish, she leaned forward and kissed me on the bare shoulder. "Invalid," she said tenderly. "Sick fancies. Morbid imagination."

"Yes," I sighed, "yes. You must be right."
"Of course I'm right."
"You're always right."
"Isn't it maddening? I always am."

Chapter Three

❖

W e were all to meet for drinks in Nigel's rooms. These were in Magdalen New Buildings, so Sue and I crossed the High Street from the hotel where we had changed; I put our suitcases into my car; and we went into the college by the main lodge. A few young men in white ties were hurrying to and fro across the front quad, and a very old scout, abstracted and muttering, shambled past us with a decanter in either hand. We went into the cloisters. A party of tourists in Fair Isle sweaters regarded us curiously; three blackbirds on the smooth turf ignored us. Turning the corner by the staircase to the Old Library, we came to the narrow arch that leads into the New Buildings quad.

"This is my favourite Oxford view," I said.

Sue looked round. "Where? These cloisters?"

"No. Wait. Walk through here."

She went into the little passage; as she saw what lay beyond she gasped.

"Isn't it perfect?"

"It's incredible," said Sue.

I followed her through the arch. It was incredible. I had expected to see, across the broad lawns, the tranquil early eighteenth-century facade of the New Buildings, beautifully imprisoned, like a picture, in the dark curved frame of the arch. In fact I saw bedlam. A huge marquee hid most of one lawn. Its extensions hid nearly everything else. Hammering sounded. Trolleys loaded with food, glasses, crockery and linen were being trundled in several directions. Workmen in shirtsleeves, who carried tools, struggled between soberly clad scouts, who carried bottles. Undergraduates in tail-coats and tennis shorts and dressing-gowns stood by, calling to each other.

"I'd forgotten this," I said.

"It's why we're here."

"Of course. I'd forgotten it, just the same."

"Golly. It does look enormous. How many people come to these things?"

"Thousands."

"Golly."

We walked gingerly among the tent pegs and the people to the shady colonnade of the New Buildings.

"What a lovely building."

"That's what I wanted you to see through that arch."

"Yes, I can imagine. It must be lovely."

"It is, as a rule. It kind of shines."

It shone now, the upper part, in the nearly horizontal sun. Strong, broken shadows from the spiky roof-line of the cloisters and the tower hit the smooth classical wall in front of us. A group of deer cantered away in the Grove beyond the ha-ha to our left. A youth with a towel round his waist ran from one staircase to another.

"We're a bit early," I said.

"Are we? Yes, we are."

"Come and see the fish."

We picked our way round the confused perimeter of the activities on the lawns, and presently stood on the little bridge that leads from the college across into Addison's Walk.

"Look," I said. "Whoppers."

We stared down at the slow stream. Among the waving reeds, and through the complicated reflections of trees and clouds and us, we could see the complacent movements of a dozen fat yellow fish.

"What sort?"

"Er—— "

"Fine guide you are, darling. They do look pleased with themselves."

"Conceited, yes."

"Arrogant I don't blame them Are you allowed to catch them?"

"Dons are."

"Do they?"

"No."

"Why not?"

"Dons don't do that sort of thing, I don't know why. They never have any fun at all."

"I'd catch them, if I was a don. But I'm glad they don't. Can we feed them?"

"They'll be fed later this evening, like fish in the English Channel."

"Don't be disgusting. Can't we get some bread?"

"Yes, I expect so. Wait here, darling."

I walked past the ludicrous Gothic lavatories of the college to the ancient cavern of the kitchens. These were full of desperate bustle: I felt it would be wrong to interrupt with a request for bread to pamper some overfed fish. But as I was quietly withdrawing, a very old man in a dirty apron caught sight of me and came limping across.

"Looking for something, sir? Just outside and on your right."

"No, no, that isn't what I'm after. Actually, I was wondering if you could spare a little bread."

"Bread, sir? There'll be a good supper, later, you know, in Hall. That is, if you're coming to the ball."

"Yes, I am, but—— "

"I guessed you were. Soon as I saw you was wearing a tail-coat, I said to myself, there's a gentleman who's—— "

"Yes, but—— "

"And actually I'm surprised, sir, that you're not dining before you ever come to the ball. It don't begin for a long time yet, you know. Most gentlemen dine before they come. That's the usual thing. Though I daresay if you had a really good luncheon—— "

"But you see, it's the fish I was thinking about—— "

"Well, sir, there'll be salmon, cold salmon. Mayonnaise there'll be with it, and then cold ham, if you fancy cold ham, sir, and cold bird—— "

"No, you don't understand, I don't mean supper—— "

"Tea, sir? I don't hardly think you'll get such a thing in college, not this evening, not at this hour. We're busy, d'you see, with all this supper I'm telling you about. I daresay if you was to pop over the High Street to the Eastgate Hotel, or it might be along the High Street to the Mitre Hotel—— "

"No *no*. I want to give the fish some bread. The fish in the river. That river."

The old man looked at me blankly. Then, very slowly, his face crumpled into a thousand wrinkles.

"Our fish! The fish under our bridge!"

"That's right!"

"You shall have bread, sir, a fine loaf of bread. A fine, fine. . . ."

He pottered off and began to peer about in the vast kitchens. Other men, old but not quite so old, bumped into him with their various burdens and hurried unnoticing on. It was at this moment that I realized the old man was drunk.

This cheered me up, I don't know why. When he came back with an immense golden loaf, I asked him to come and feed the fish with us.

He looked round furtively, then turned to me with a happy, mad smile.

"Yes, sir," he said, "yes. I'd like that. Really I would. It's the first time—will you believe me, sir, it's the first time a young gentleman has ever asked me to go and feed the fish with 'um. Oh, I'd like that."

"Come on, then."

I walked very slowly towards the bridge so that the old man could keep up with me. When we had nearly covered the thirty-yard course he stopped and looked at me.

"I wonder if *one*—— "

"What?"

"I just thought—I wonder if *one*—— "

"What?"

"Wait here, sir, will you?" he said with sudden energy. "And hold this bread, if you'll be so kind—— "

He gave me the great oblong loaf and started tacking back along the gravel path. I lit a cigarette and waited. After a long pause he reappeared, holding in his ancient arms two more immense loaves.

"Here we are, sir. We'll give our fish a meal they'll remember. This'll be a red-letter evening for our fish, this will. Why, I don't 'spect they've ever had a meal like this one we're going to give them, not in all their lives."

"No, I don't expect they have—— "

When we got to the bridge, I and my old bread-bearer, Sue had disappeared. There were three enormous backs turned to me and I realized, presently, that Sue was behind them.

"Sue—— "

"Oh darling, what a long time you've been."

168

"But look what I've got."

"Darling! A huge meal!"

"That's right, miss," said the old man, grinning with delight, "a yuge meal is right."

"It sure is," said one of the broad backs, now a broad front with a crew-cut and a camera.

"It sure's hell is."

"We've given them some hors-d'œuvre," said Sue. "Some delicious Charleston Chew."

"Some *what*?"

"Charleston Chew. Very gooey."

"Candy," explained one of the immense Americans. "Kind of a candy-bar. You oughta try it. Only thing, we don't have any more."

"Fish ate it all."

"They sure did."

"They loved it," said Sue.

"They sure's hell did."

"Well, I hope it's given them an appetite," I said. "They've got a lot of bread to get through."

"C'mon, let's get to breaking it up. Gotta break it up, see, and then drop it down in there."

"That's right. Gotta be broken up first."

"All right. You break this one up—— "

"An' I'll break this one up—— "

"By the way," said Sue, "this is my husband. He's called Eddie. This is Hal and this is Chick and this is, er—— "

"Schroeder."

"Schroeder, of course."

"How do you do?"

"Glad to know you, Eddie."

"Great to meet you, Eddie."

"Hi."

"Hi," I said.

"Say, Sue, is this the fight kind of a size chunk to give them?"

"That's about it, Chick."

"Great. O.K. let's go."

"Wait it, Chick," said Hal. "Let's get a little simultaneity into this. Let's get a little co-ordination."

"Yeah, that's right. You give the word."

"All ready? Let's go!"

Hunks of bread, somewhat larger than a man's hand, rained down on to the smooth, water. The fat fish boiled about hysterically. The three Americans grinned and tore off more chunks. The old man from the kitchen jumped up and down in his excitement, shredding fragments off his loaf and dropping them casually on to the stone parapet.

"Hold it, there," cried Hal with authority. "Hold it, boys. Give them time to get around that lot before we give them another consignment."

"Check," said Schroeder.

"Check," said Sue.

As we watched, the chunks of bread became smaller and smaller as fragments were torn off them by dozens, now, of greedy yellow fish. Presently the troubled water smoothed and the fish lay quietly "on the fin", waiting for whatever new breadfall this amazing evening should bring.

Hal raised a hand. "Stand by."

Chick, Schroeder, the old man, Sue and I stood by.

"Start breading!"

We began again. The Americans gave great bellows of laughter. Sue was giggling helplessly. The old man was beside himself with glee.

In the next pause—ordered, this time, by Schroeder—I glanced at my watch.

"Sue, we ought to go to Nigel's."

"Yes, all right." She turned to the others. "We've got to go I'm afraid."

"Is that so? That's bad."

"That's certainly too bad."

"Well, it's been great to meet you, Sue, Eddie—— "

"Good to have known you, Eddie, Sue—— "

"So long."

"So long," I said.

We shook hands warmly all round—Sue also taking affectionate farewell of the old man—and retraced our careful steps round the lawns and over to the New Buildings. As we approached, a window shot up on the second floor.

"Hi!"

"Hullo, Nigel. Are we late?"

"No, early."

"Oh dear. Too early?"

"Far too early. Come on up."

"You wouldn't rather we went away and came back later?"

"No no. Come up and have a drink. I'll be dressing."

"All right."

We went up the battered oak stairs. Nigel was waiting, half-dressed but very elegant in a silk dressing-gown, on his landing.

"Come on in. Lots of Charley."

"Charley?"

"Charley gold-top." He indicated a large number of champagne bottles standing in a tin bath.

"Oh—I see. How marvellous. Shall I open one?"

"One open. I tried to hit a tripper with the cork. Low angle shot, rather tricky. Missed, I'm afraid."

Sue looked out of the window down on to the crowded quad.

"I bet you hit *someone*" she said.

"Only on the bounce. Hardly counts."

"N-no. How did you manage not to spill all the champagne?"

"I did spill some, I must admit. Hit someone with that, all right."

"How awful."

"Well, it was only a don."

"How *awful*."

"No no," said Nigel tolerantly. "He was rather pleased. He's the sort of don who likes to feel he's one of the boys."

"That was lucky."

"Well, yes. Anyway, there's plenty left. Glasses, now where are those damned glasses?"

"Those ones?"

"Oh yes, good. I think I'd better finish dressing, if you'll excuse me. When you finish this lot of Charley, do open some more."

"All right," I said. "Thanks."

"We'll try and hit a tripper with the cork."

"*Do.*"

Nigel disappeared into his bedroom and Sue and I settled down.

He had clearly gone to a lot of trouble. Besides all the champagne in the improvised cooler, there were flowers stacked in vases on tables and bookshelves; cigarettes in cups and boxes; a great number of oddly assorted ashtrays; food of all sorts—strawberries, cold meat, little *vol-au-vents*, biscuits, cakes, fruit—ranged on a table by one of the big windows; and a tremendous absence of papers, books and garments which, in an undergraduate's sitting-room, almost always means recent and strenuous tidying.

Presently other people began to arrive. Nigel's partner first, then Jonathan and Clare; then four young men, all with girls; then three young men without girls; then some girls; then Christopher and Mary Massingham; then some others. It became a considerable party.

The casuals (so to call them) left fairly soon: they were all going to the ball and they all had places where they had to be. Though this exodus left ten of us still in the room, it seemed very quiet and intimate. The hammering and bustling outside had at last stopped. A few couples walked slowly over the bridge where we had fed the fish, or stopped to stare at the huge marquee where they would, a few hours later, spend so many hours. It was the lull between the time when everybody was getting ready for the evening and the time when the evening started.

I well remember the look of our party in this quiet phase. In the window by the food-table, Nigel and Sue stood looking out and talking quietly. He pointed out some feature of the old part of the college opposite; she nodded, turned to him to smile briefly at something he said, and then followed his pointing arm in another direction. On the big black leather sofa sat three girls: Nigel's partner Sarah, Tim's partner Caroline, and Mary. Tim sat on one arm, Jonathan on the other. Jonathan and Tim were discussing, rather desultorily, the recent form in the county cricket championship. Mary was looking into the middle distance. The other two girls were gossiping quietly. Following Mary's eyes, I looked at Christopher. He was sitting by himself in the far window, smoking and looking down into the quad below.

Beside me sat Clare. She was wearing a very pale blue dress with an enormous skirt, on which, here and there, something glittered. She had long, drop diamond ear-rings (a wedding present, I knew) and a very beautiful diamond necklace (Jonathan's mother's, I think). Her fair hair shone brilliantly in the gentle light. She was asking me about Grasse and the mountains and our farm; her face was mildly animated; she spoke quietly; she seemed to me to be smoking a good deal, but she drank almost nothing. I remember admitting to myself, exactly as the weird bells of Magdalen chimed eight o'clock, that she was after all definitely beautiful.

Nigel came over from the window to fill our glasses. Clare covered hers with her hand; I proffered mine.

"Really, Clare?"

"Yes, really, thank you, Nigel."

"Perhaps you'd like something different? A cocktail of some kind? Sherry? I'm not sure how the commissariat's fixed, but it's the easiest thing in the word to—— "

"No, really not. I'll tell you, shall I, when I want some more?"

"Well, can I rely on you to tell me the *moment* you want some more?"

"Yes, honestly, I promise."

"Good. You'll have to make sure Clare keeps that promise," he said to me.

"I will," I said.

He moved to the sofa and began filling glasses there.

"I like Nigel," said Clare.

"So do I."

Clare and I had never had very much to say to each other: at this point we had nothing. But our silence was not really uncomfortable: we just didn't say anything.

I looked round the room again.

Christopher was where he had been, by himself in the window. Jonathan, still on the arm of the sofa, was talking to the girls nearer him. I overheard the name Daniel Gelin, the name Gerard, the name Tati. Tim had moved over to talk to Sue in the other window. Nigel, as I watched, filled his own glass and carried it into his bedroom. I looked at Mary Massingham. To my surprise I thought she was staring at me. But I realized after a moment that she was staring at Clare. She caught my eye and immediately looked down and away. When I looked at her a moment later she was staring at Christopher.

I thought: something's up. I thought: something's wrong.

Chapter Four

❖

W e dined gaily and well in Woodstock. The ten of us sat round an enormous table in an enormous dining-room. All about us, round other enormous tables, other enormous parties dined. On my left sat Sarah, Nigel's pretty little partner; on my right sat Mary Massingham. Beyond Sarah there was Jonathan, and beyond Mary, Nigel's agreeable, indeterminate friend Tim. Clare was opposite me, between Nigel and Christopher: as we sat down she smiled at me across a fathom of white linen, a bowl of carnations, and a lot of glasses and spoons. I decided again that she was beautiful, and I smiled back. Then I began to wonder who had arranged the seating. Then, luckily, I had to answer polite questions from Sarah about my own unspectacular Oxford career.

"No, I didn't hunt. Not even with the Drag. I beagled sometimes. Well, in my first year, anyway."

"Is that fun?"

"Ghastly."

"You run?"

"Run and run."

"Ghastly, yes. . . . But didn't you belong to any of those clubs with pretty coats that bust up bicycles after dinner?"

"I was the man that owned the bicycles."

"All of them?"

"Most of them."

"Oh. . . ."

"Quite a gay evening last Wednesday," said a high voice behind me. "We festooned bicycles on every lamp-post in whatever that funny street is called."

"The Turl," said a similar voice.

"What a quaint name," said a girl's voice that sounded familiar. "Is it a nice street?"

"I really don't know, Angie. I've never been down it in the daytime."

I turned round. A party had just sat down at the next huge table, which was already strewn with magnums. From the long fair hair of the first speaker (a soft-faced youth with a spot on his neck) came a heady waft of Trumper's Coronis.

"No bicycle is safe," giggled Sarah.

"Ah, the gay young blades—— "

"I expect he's quite nice really."

"I expect he will be one day."

"Will you forgive me," she said, "if I say that you sound a tiny bit pompous?"

"No," I said, "I won't."

"Oh dear."

"But only because you're right. Isn't it awful? I'm quite young really."

"You *look* about seventeen."

"That's my tragedy. It's because of my fine red face."

"It *is* red. But it's very honest."

"Yes, isn't it awful?"

"Hullo, Nigel," cried the fair youth. "I was telling Angie about our bicycle-hunt."

"Hullo, Robin. You mustn't shout about it. We'll get into terrible trouble."

"Oh tush."

"Perkins," I laughed without thinking. Then I caught Clare's eye. "Sorry."

She smiled. "That's all right. Even Adrian doesn't take himself really seriously."

"Doesn't he? I never knew that."

"Well, he doesn't either, altogether."

"Your brother, darling," said Jonathan, "is—— "

"Shh, Uncle Jonathan," said Christopher. "No shop. It's bad enough to have that terrible old Major bragging about his doggish days as an Undergrad—— "

"He wasn't," said Sarah. "He was apologizing for them."

"I found myself apologizing for not being a dog," I said. "Most odd it felt. Shows what environment will do."

"Ooh you wicked fraud," said Christopher. "I will tell you about him, Sarah. He was a terror. The terror of the Turl. Where others bent bicycles, he destroyed cars. Many's the Austin Seven I have striven to save—— "

"You, darling?" said Sue. "I don't believe it."

"But you must, Sue. Now it can be told, I expect, the truth about your husband—— "

"Oh Robin," came Angelica's voice, "you *didn't*—— "

"Certainly. And the Proctor was quite civil, poor little man. Rather a snob, I suspect—— "

"Consommé, Madame?"

"Oh, thank you—— "

We were very merry. That is to say, Jonathan was, and I was, and Sue was, and Nigel and Sarah and Tim and Caroline were. Clare was never a one for fierce gaiety (her fierceness was of a different kind) but she was, I thought, enjoying herself. Mary was a little subdued, but I expect she found me dull. But Christopher—I had never seen Christopher in such form. I thought, at first, that he was a little drunk: perhaps he was, but only a very little. He was almost wild; there was something furious in his high spirits; it was tremendous fun sitting opposite to him and getting the full blast of his enjoyment. When they cleared away the small, deep soup-bowls, he began spinning his knife on the shiny mat (a print of Haddon Hall) in front of him.

"The person this points to is the biggest bully in the fourth," he cried.

Slowly it decelerated, and waveringly stopped midway between Mary and me.

"Oh you rotters!"

"No no," I said, and gestured backwards: the knife pointed at the elegant back of the fair young man with the spot.

"Oh no, Major. He's only in the Remove."

I laughed and caught Angelica's eye. She turned and whispered something to her neighbour, who tittered and glanced at me.

Christopher spun his knife again. "The person this points to is a frightful silly stupid ass, and will break a suspender during a waltz at one a.m."

Less smoothly swung this time, the knife wobbled more rapidly to a halt: and pointed at Christopher.

"Liar," he said. "False prophet. The person *this* points to is a sickening ghastly terrible stinker and bounder and not to be trusted by anyone."

Again his spin was false. Again the knife rattled to an unsteady halt to point directly at Christopher's lower shirt-stud.

"It's obviously right," said Clare.

"Of course it is," said Sue. "Omens don't lie. Oh *Christopher—* "

He hung his head. "I'm exposed. Sir Jasper Townsend, notorious in three parishes — "

"Two," said Mary unexpectedly.

He glanced up. "Yes, small time stuff really. . . . Now the

179

person *this* points to is brilliant and popular and will be incredibly successful and is Man Most Likely to Succeed."

He flicked hard, and the shining knife looked like a many-spoked wheel on the table. Our next course, a bird, was being served: but the waiter hung behind Christopher's chair with a half-grin, unwilling to interrupt the pantomime. Very gradually the knife lost speed; when it was travelling slowly it still revolved, like a roulette-wheel, long after one thought it must stop. Hardly moving, the point swung past Mary, me, Sarah, Jonathan, Sue, and—infinitely slowly—Nigel and Clare. It stopped exactly as it had stopped before.

Christopher bowed slightly to left and right. "Thank you, thank you."

"Loaded wheel," said Jonathan. "Crook."

"A prophet is seldom honoured—— "

"Excuse me, sir—— "

"Ah, how delicious—a prophet *is* honoured—— "

"Rather touching," came a high voice from behind me.

"Hush, Robin," said Angelica.

"Have you got everything you want, Mary?" I asked.

"Mm? I don't know. . . ."

"Hullo, Mary," said a girl's quiet voice.

"Hullo, Clarissa. My cousin," she explained to me. "She married that man—— "

"Jeremy, yes I know him."

A party of four had arrived at another nearby table: Jeremy Laxton, a severe-faced young broker (I think) or banker; his very pretty, slightly waif-like wife; a man I had known quite well at the University called Henry Fenwick, whom I saw in London occasionally at parties of a kind he enjoyed more than I did (he was in advertising, working for a large, rich, rather discredited firm); and, evidently with Henry, a red-haired girl to whom he now introduced me as Jenny something.

"Hello, Christopher," Jeremy was saying. "I thought you were in America?"

"He is," said Henry. "Certainly he is."

"You're absolutely right," said Christopher, "I am."

"Are you back?"

"How foolish," said Henry, "can a question get?"

"There are no limits, Henry. Oblige me by trying to fix no limits."

"Come on," said Jenny. "Let's sit down and eat, don't you think?"

"See you all later," said Mary.

"You'll find it difficult not to see us now."

"But possible, Henry, possible," said Christopher.

"Can you make a thing you dislike just disappear, Christopher?" said Clare.

"I can make Henry Fenwick disappear. I can make him so that he never existed."

"I doubt if he ever did," I said.

"That may be. That may well be."

"Poor man," said Sue. "He looks all right."

"He is all right," admitted Christopher. "At least he used to be. Is he still, Major?"

"He will be, I think."

"There you go again, pompous," said Sarah. "I don't know Henry very well, but I think he's very nice, and, er—— "

"Yes," I said, "yes."

Presently Christopher lifted his glass of *vin rosé* and stared at me, portentously, through it. Again I wondered if he had drunk too much; again I decided that he hadn't.

"There was a young person named Eddie, whose wit was a trifle unready—— "

"As a gay undergrad, his manners were bad—— " said Sarah.

"But his habits were horribly steady. Isn't that good?"

"Brilliant."

"A well-chosen word, my dear Clare. That knife did not lie. There was a young lady named Clare, the chief of whose charms was her hair—— "

"It started as black," I said.

"She detected a lack," said Sue.

"So it finished unswervingly fair," said Christopher.

"That's rude, Christopher."

"The Major's fault. Ungallantry lurks like a scorpion, you know, behind that deceptively rosy brow."

"Nark," said Sue. "Scab. Blame-shifter."

"There was a young *woman* named Sue, whose virtues were viciously few—— "

"There was a young fellow named Townsend," replied Sue quickly.

"I bet you can't finish that."

"Who, er—— "

"Ten to one against."

"Taken," I said.

"Who, er—— "

"Quids?" said Christopher.

"Certainly."

"Who was chased all the way to the town's end—— "

"Oh cheat."

"Not a bit of it," I said. "Most ingenious. It goes on—— "

"Before you begin, let me specify the plot-line," said Christopher. "This young person you name so awkwardly in your ill-constructed doggerel, Sue, is chased, if at all, by a horde of beautiful, insanely jealous women fighting bitterly among themselves for his favours or even a glance. A glance," he repeated, emptying his glass and immediately refilling it.

"Who was chased all the way to the town's end—" said Sue.

"By a phalanx of duns," said Jonathan.

"Phalanx, what a lovely word."

"With a number of guns—— "

"No," said Mary. "He was quite right about the plot. He was chased all the way to the town's end, by a bevy of beauty intent on the duty of making him bow to their gowns' end."

"Splendid," said Jonathan. "Serve him right."

I glanced at Mary. She had returned to her plate, and was separating meat from a complicated bone with devoted, even excessive, attention. For some reason there was an embarrassing pause.

"That girl with Henry Fenwick," I said, making conversation, "do you know her?"

"Jenny? Yes. She's all right."

"I thought there was another girl—— "

"There was. As a matter of fact she's over there—— "

I followed her indications and saw, at the other end of the room, a thin fair face listening without expression to a many-gestured conversation between the excited men who sat each side of her at the corner table.

"Poor Henry," I said.

"Up to a point."

"That's a bit hard."

"Yes. . . ."

The party at the smaller of our neighbour tables was very quiet, I noticed, in contrast to the exuberance of ours and the other large one. Henry, as I saw out of the corner of my eye, was looking in every direction except the corner where the fair girl still sat silently listening to the conversations round her. He caught my eye and absently half-waved. Jeremy Laxton was eating smoked salmon with gloomy concentration. Clarissa, his small and, as I now saw, pregnant wife, talked often but it seemed rather hopelessly. Jenny, the red-haired girl, was quite unconcerned by the evident wrongness of this particular dinner-party; she prattled gaily and very audibly:

"Goodness, Anglica has got some awful people in her party—one very glamorous man, though, I must admit, at least he would be if he hadn't got that spot, or is that bitchy?—and what fun they are having next door, Mary and Christopher and those people—who is that very beautiful man with long grey hair, and look at those ear-rings, goodness——"

"A tiny morgue," I heard the 'glamorous man' say, "d'you see, Angie? They're laid out on slabs. Fenwick, did you say that man was called? Dead for days. I pity that red-haired sweetie——"

"Oh, Jenny, she's all right."

"That's what I mean."

"Robin, is that polite?"

"Polite? you wouldn't want me being polite——"

"Coffee, sir?"

"Oh yes," I said, "thanks."

"Brandy, Major?"

"Yes please, Christopher."

"Careful, darling."

"Oh *Sue*," said Jonathan.

"Golly, did I really say 'careful'? How awful——"

"I know just how you feel," said Clare.

"So do I," said Mary.

"Ah, wait till you're married."

"I am."

"Married? You never told us——"

"No, waiting."

"With ill-concealed impatience," said someone. I felt at the time the joke was a mistake, although no flicker on Mary's face gave any indication that she had even heard it.

"Ought we to move?" said Tim.

"Heavens no. Far too early."

"Can we just sit?"

"Bored?"

"No no. But they will like it?"

"Who, the waiters?"

"Yes."

"Loathe it, I expect," said Nigel. "We'll sit here a bit, don't you think, Uncle Jonathan, and then trickle back?"

"Yes, I should think so."

"Terrible to arrive just when the band's tuning up."

"Do they tune up? I suppose they must, of course. What agony."

"Agony if they didn't."

"Agony to turn up and see acres of empty floor. One's embarrassed laugh echoing through hundreds of yards of deserted canvas—— "

"Yes, what a terrifying picture you do paint, Nigel, to be sure. Let's by all means wait. We'd all better have some more brandy. Sarah?"

"Yes please."

"Mary?"

"No thank you."

"Do," I said.

"A good idea, do you think?" she asked me. "Yes, I expect you're right. It's so nasty, that's the only thing."

"Have something else."

"No, brandy will do."

"Got a matchbox, Major?" said Christopher suddenly.

"No."

"Of course, you use a terrible lighter."

"My lighter is not terrible. All agree about the beauty of its finish, the dependability of its action—— "

"You've been reading advertisements, that's your trouble."

"I've got some," said Sarah, "a book."

"No good," said Christopher. "Abox, I require. No boxes?"

"Yes," said Mary, "here."

She threw the box inexpertly across the table: it looked as though it must land in Clare's glass, but Christopher dextrously caught it with a quick movement. Not tight, I realized. Not tight at all.

He put the box on the table in front of him, and stuck a match, head upwards, through the thin wood of the top. then he leant another match, head upwards, against the first.

"The perfect kiss," he announced. "You've never seen anything like this."

"Oh *no*—— " I said.

"Please, Major, stop jogging the table. In fact, I must ask you all to take your arms, elbows and shoulders off the table and sit perfectly still. Now. Watch."

With his own lighter he set fire to the leaning match, near the bottom. We all watched, most of us smiling expectantly. The small flame grew bigger, running up the inclined stick of the match. Suddenly the two heads flared up, almost simultaneously. Then the flame dwindled and crept down the vertical match.

"Here we go," said Christopher. "The perfect kiss."

As he spoke, the absurd, convincing symbolism I had seen so often before happened: the leaning match quivered, began to bend, and then raised its lower end in a series of spasmodic, almost orgasmic twitches. It did look (as this wonderful trick always does look) exactly like a passionate kiss.

We all laughed—nearly all of us.

"*Won*derful," said Sarah.

"Bliss."

"Wow," said Tim. "Do it again."

"Did you hear that? Oh, you saucy boy—— "

"No, do, Christopher," said Sue. "It killed me."

"All right. The perfect kiss—— "

As, again, the leaning match flared and then bent and heaved Clare began to laugh consumedly.

"Vicarious pleasure," said Christopher, shaking his head. "Worrying, that."

"What's that mean?"

"This is a highly unsuitable exhibition, Christopher," said Jonathan. "I feel like the butler, quite guilty."

"Then you don't feel like the butler."

"I feel like someone walking through Hyde Park on a summer evening," said Sue.

"Like a man in a punt going past other punts," said Nigel.

"Not even *other* punts, if you remember, Nigel," said Tim.

"Quiet, Judas."

"What's that, Tim?" said Sarah. "Tell me. I ought to know—— "

"No no," said Tim. "Later, pethaps."

"How does it make *you* feel, Clare?" said Mary.

But Clare was still laughing, and did not reply.

"Goodness," I heard Jenny say, "what a good idea. Have you got any matches, Henry?"

"What?"

"Matches, darling. A box of matches. For that kiss thing."

"What?"

"Quite reminds me of happy hours in the Naafi," said the youth called Robin. "When I was a recruit."

"I think it's heaven," said Angelica. "Have you got any matches?"

"No."

"I'll get some. Waiter—— "

"Oh Angie—— "

"It's heaven."

"Now I think perhaps we might make a move," said Jonathan.

"All right."

"How shall we go? As we came? Or split up?"

"Split up."

"Yes, split up."

"All right. Who'll come with me?"

"Me, Jonathan," said Sue, "please."

"All right, Sue, delighted. And you, Nigel? And Caroline?"

"Yes, good, thanks."

"Oh, that wonderful car? *Good——* "

"Come with me, Mary?" I said.

"Thank you."

"May I?" said Tim, "and Sarah?"

"Yes, do. Come on. Who does that leave?"

But before the question had been considered we seemed to be in the car and trying, quite vainly, to keep up with Jonathan. Clare, of course (I then remembered): and Christopher, of course.

"Shall we go straight to Nigel's room and organize?"

"Presently we must. A godsend to have a base," said Tim. "Nothing worse than drifting all night. Actually, I feel like a dance after all that scoff. Caroline?"

"Love to."

"What about you, Mary?" I said.

"All right."

We had arrived at a good time. The huge dance-floor was full, but not yet packed. There was nobody drunk that I could see. The noise was terrific but not quite deafening. By far the most sedate people were a few well-scrubbed Americans, prominent on account of their white tuxedos, The undergraduates, about two-thirds of whom were in white ties, had a tendency at this stage to jive (which they did badly) or swoop about in a grotesque but not ungraceful exaggeration of the night-club glide to which, over the past few years, I had become more or less accustomed. Through the wide flaps of the open end of the main marquee a cool breeze, already grateful, fitfully moved: it stirred paper napkins and loose, soft locks of hair, principally those of men. Mary and I rather demurely shuffled round the edge, threading our silent way through couples half dancing, half standing talking (the man generally talking to another man with loud bursts of not altogether easy laughter, the girl jigging to the music, anxious to take wings). Mary's scent was slight but pleasant; when we quick-stepped past the edge of the warm, pale night there was a much stronger, sweeter scent from the gardens.

"It'll be a hopeless scrum soon," I said.

"Yes?"

"But then it'll thin down. And then later there'll be so much dew on the floor—this part, anyway, near the door—that you won't be able to slide at all."

"No."

"But I was forgetting—you know all about these things."

"Yes."

She was not easy to talk to.

"What about a drink?"

"No, I didn't think so, thank you. But you have one."

"Oh no—Shall we go back to Nigel's?"

"All right."

We crossed the narrow, crowded strip of quad between the marquee and the New Buildings colonnade, and I saw that a moon was rising weirdly over the trees. We stopped to look at it. The gay, harsh noise of the band, dominated at this distance by the insistent thump-thump of the drums; the muffled roar of several hundred voices; the moonlight; the heavy mood of the girl beside me: all these combined to produce the most complicated emotions in me.

"Come on," I finally said, "we'll have some champagne."

"All right."

Chapter Five

✣

An hour later, soon after midnight, I was dancing with Sue. She was wearing a light green dress which flattered the soft hazel of her eyes; her slimness was scarcely yet disturbed by the baby; her small face was full of gaiety. I felt a rush of tenderness—of golden, undeserved good fortune. Other people—Mary, Clare, Henry Fenwick—had problems, it seemed; but Sue and I were all right. We were the favourites of the naughty gods. Nothing could touch us.

"O Sue," I said.

"What?"

"How I do love you."

She smiled. "Good."

I pulled her towards me and we danced cheek to cheek, slowly, along the cool open end of the floor.

"How stiff your shirt is, darling."

"It's a stiff shirt."

"That must be it."

"Do the studs dig into you?"

"Yes. I shall be all bruises."

"Oh dear," I said, "people will misunderstand."

"Not really. Do I dig into you?"

"Yes, lovely. I shall be all bruises."

"Never mind, darling," she said, "people will understand."

"Hullo, Sue," said someone.

"Hullo, Tim. Hullo, Caroline. Isn't this nice?"

"Very nice. All cool here."

"Nice smell."

"Yes, what are those flowers?"

"They're yellow. I noticed them this morning. Lovely pong."

"Sorry," said a man.

"Oh, sorry—— "

"Where's that girl?" said a man. "Where's that dam' girl?"

"I don't know," I said. "Which girl?"

"No one you know." He looked at me owlishly. "You keep out of this."

"All right."

"That's better."

He stumbled out on to the lawn. "Marigold! Marigold, Damn it!"

"Honkers."

"Poor man. Pushed."

"A thought pushed. Beastly Marigold."

"I can see Marigold," said Tim, "can't you?"

"Brassy," said Sue.

"Sequins."

"High laugh. Talks about Non-U. Flat in Basil Street."

"Model?"

"No, secretary in the Foreign Office."

"Ghastly."

"Ghastly," agreed Tim. "Well, I think I'm thirsty."

"Good-bye."

"Good-bye," said Caroline. "Have a nice time."

"Hullo," said a red-haired girl: Jenny, I remembered.

"Hullo," I said. "Oh, hullo, Henry."

"This end is nice," said Jenny. "You are clever to have found this end. Let's stay this end, darling."

"All right," said Henry. "We can look at the moon."

"By the light of the silvery moon," sang Jenny, quite loudly, against whatever the band was playing.

"*La lune ne garde aucune rancune,*" said Henry, "unlike some."

"You're being rather acid. Why are you being so acid? He's being acid," she told us, "I think he thinks it suits him."

"He looks well on it," said Sue.

"Do I?"

"Very smart," I said.

"Acid," said Jenny again. "You need some Alka-Seltzer or something. Eno's."

The music stopped. Jenny, Sue and I clapped.

"Let's go and look at those fish again," said Sue.

"Yes."

"You'd better have some shampoo, darling," said Jenny.

"Shampoo?"

"Champagne."

"Oh I see," said Sue, "yes, of course."

"Come on, darling," I said.

"Good-bye," said Jenny. "See you later, probably."

"Yes."

We walked hand in hand to the bridge and leaned over the parapet. The moon had climbed high enough to light the stonework, and our silhouetted reflections, a single, two-headed black shape, loomed curiously up at us from the smooth water.

"No fish," said a girl's voice. "I thought you said there were fish."

"It's too dark to see them," said a man. "There are dozens."

"Make them appear."

"How, for God's sake? Be reasonable, Antonia."

"Make them appear."

"You know, darling," I said quietly, "there's something odd going on tonight."

"What do you mean? The fish not appearing?"

"Not the fish. In our party."

"It's a very nice party. Very nice people."

"Yes. Christopher drove Clare back from Woodstock."

"She couldn't very well have walked. Too far. Wrong sort of shoes."

"You know what I mean."

"You're barmy, darling. Honestly you're dotty. Do stop putting two and two together and making seventeen. I asked Jonathan to take me, and then Jonathan asked Nigel and Caroline. You were there, you must remember. Then you asked some people. That left Clare. Christopher had to take her. You're putting two and two together and making thirty-one."

"Four's enough to worry hell out of me."

"You're dotty. What *have* you seen?"

"Nothing, exactly, but—— "

"No. What you need is a drink, you dirty-minded old Turk."

"I hope to God you're right."

"Come on, darling. Shamrock. No, that isn't quite what she called it—— "

"Shampoo."

"That's right. Not very funny, really, is it?"

"Not very,"

"Let's go and have some, even so."

"All right."

"Hullo. Have some strawberries."

"Hullo, Nigel. Yes, lovely. Woof," Sue sat down with a sigh on the sofa.

"Charley?"

"Lovely."

Mary was sitting in an armchair, leaning far back and staring at the ceiling. There was an empty glass in her hand, which Nigel filled. Caroline and Tim were talking quietly in the far window, where Christopher had sat by himself five hours earlier.

"Where are the others?"

"Dancing, I suppose, or pottering about. Uncle Jonathan went off with Sarah just now."

"Christopher?"

"Haven't seen him for hours. Pottering about, I suppose.'"

"Or dancing."

"Yes. Charley, Eddie?"

"Yes, thanks."

The muffled music of the band came now thumpity-thumpity from below: a waltz. I imagined the brilliant swirl on the dance-floor: the reddened, damp faces of the men, with locks of hair collapsing down over their right eyes: the set half-smiles of vigorously revolving girls: the splendid billowing of full skirts rising as they spun. This picture was nice, but I was glad to be in Nigel's comfortable, dim-lit room, lying back in the soft black leather sofa beside Sue, sipping champagne and dunking big, moist strawberries into a bowl of sugar.

"This is nice."

"Isn't it?" said Sue. "You are clever, Nigel, to have this nice room and these nice strawberries and this nice cham-pagne and those nice candles—— "

"Aren't I? I wish Uncle Jonathan would come back with Sarah. I've hardly seen her since dinner."

"Mm?"

"He's got a wife of his own. Pinching my cookie—— "

"I doubt it," said Sue. "Not Jonathan. Not on the dance-floor."

Nigel laughed. "Patting, perhaps."

"Or petting."

"Don't be disgusting."

"A wife of his own, has he?" said Mary. "Yes. Can I have some more champagne, Nigel, please?"

"God I'm sorry, how rude of me, of course—— "

"Moon," said Caroline from the window to Sue, "have you seen?"

"Yes, heaven."

"Tim," said Nigel, "would it be very tactless if I asked Caroline to dance?"

"Yes," said Tim.

"No," said Caroline. She turned to Tim and put a hand on his. "I'll be back. Don't jump out of the window."

"I may, if you're away too long."

"Keep at the Charley, Tim."

"Yes, console myself—— "

"Have some cake too, then," said Caroline, "you sot."

"Blotch, do I need? As a matter of fact I do feel rather like a bit of delicious cake."

"Pig."

"Don't be long."

"No, I promise."

"Keep at the Charley, Eddie."

"All right, thanks."

Caroline and Nigel left, and the four of us sat quietly for a minute.

"Champagne, Mary?"

"Yes please . . . thank you."

"Sue," said Tim, "would you like to dance?"

"Love to."

"Splendid. They've been doing one of those terrible waltz things, but they seem to have settled down again."

"Oh good."

"Come on, then."

"Mary?" I said.

"What?"

"Dance?"

"Oh. . . . No, I don't think so, thanks."

"All right."

Presently she stood up and moved vaguely over to the window. She leaned forward so that her forehead rested on the glass of the wide-open lower panes: she looked, against the brilliant moonlight, like a Victorian silhouette of a pensive nymph.

"I'm afraid you're not having a very good time," I said.

"What? No, not very. Don't let me be a bore."

"You're not. Er—— "

"Don't try and comfort me, for God's sake."

"All right."

She turned quickly. "I'm sorry. I didn't mean to sound as shrill as that. But you know what I mean."

"Yes, I know."

After a moment she said, "You know that feeling you sometimes have, when you're ill, that the one thing you can't bear is anyone talking about it or being sympathetic?"

"I know."

"You feel like screaming when people say 'poor thing'."

"I know. I wasn't going to say 'poor thing'."

"Weren't you?" She looked at me dubiously. "Weren't you? Oh good." I filled my glass from the half-full bottle on the floor at my feet: then, seeing her empty glass in her hand, I got up and went over to her.

"Thank you. I don't really frightfully like this stuff—— "

"Too fizzy?"

"Rather fizzy. And sort of—vulgar-tasting. Never mind." She took a large sip. "Christopher's a great friend of yours, isn't he?"

"Yes he is."

"Yes. He's often told me about you."

"Oh? What's he been saying about me?"

"Well, you know what people say about people. He said you were nice. Are you nice? Yes, you are, I think. He said you were frightfully honest."

"Oh good. So's he, I think, don't you?"

"Do you?" she said, "do you?"

"Of course," I said, "I don't quite know what. . . . This evening seems odd—— "

"A bit odd. Shall I go and drown myself, or would that be silly?"

"A bit silly."

"I expect you're right. It would be nice, though."

"Have some champagne."

"All right. Two months ago I thought I was the happiest—— "

"Oh," I said uneasily. "He's very gay, and—— "

"Very gay. Very sweet, he was. Very happy, I was. Very silly, I was, too. Because this started happening weeks ago, this. . . . He'd be somewhere else, you know what I mean? Always somewhere else—— "

"Withdrawn."

"Out of sight. A million miles away. Space-fiction distance."

"He's been very busy," I said. "Are you sure it isn't just because he's been so busy? You couldn't believe what sort of time he's been having at the office—quite crazy, very worrying—— "

"Yes, he told me. That's not it."

"Are you sure? He's been doing all this television business—a new thing, very difficult—— "

"That's not it."

"Are you sure? Can you be sure? Everything may be perfectly—— "

197

"Of course I'm sure. Can't you see that? Of course I'm sure."

"Yes," I admitted.

"I'm sorry to bore you like this."

"You're not," I said again. "I wish I could help."

"Ah, well, help. Can I take you up on asking me to dance?"

"Of course."

"I must move about, I think—— "

But when we got to the dance-floor and saw the packed, swaying crowd she said: "Perhaps not, do you think, after all?"

"All right. Rather a nightmare."

"They're all so merry."

They didn't all look merry. Many faces wore the intensely concentrated, remotely abstracted look of dancers into whose gyrations sex is powerfully entering. One girl, looking over the lightly-powdered black shoulder of her partner, yawned with wide-mouthed abandon. One purplish youth, who had both his arms round the waist of a tall, unhappy-looking girl, hiccupped audibly as he rocked past.

"Let's go for a walk," said Mary. "A short walk. Show me the college. Were you at this college?"

"Yes."

"Show me the beauty-spots."

"All right. We'll go and look at the cloisters. They ought to look nice in this moon."

"Ridiculous moon."

"Tactless moon?"

"Very tactless, very tasteless, very vulgar moon."

We walked round the cloisters and I told her about the Gladstone and Disraeli gargoyles. It was pretty: but the cloisters were too crowded for her melancholy mood. Two dozen couples were strolling round as we were. Laughter sounded from open windows. A scout with a tray edged past a noisy group at the foot of a staircase.

So we went to the bridge. Once again I found myself staring at my dark reflection.

"It was that hole in your sock—— "

This surprising remark, from a girl's husky voice behind me, made me glance round. A couple were leaning on the other parapet, a yard apart, talking quietly.

"The rain," said the man.

"The bus."

"Oh darling—— "

It was Henry Fenwick, I realized, the unhappy man whose red-haired partner Jenny had been trying so hard to have a good time.

"I went to my flat," said the girl, "and I sat in a chair for six hours—— " This was not Jenny. Was it the fair girl Mary had pointed out to me?

"You sat looking at the rain—— "

"Yes. It got dark. I went to bed in the end."

"October—— "

I turned to Mary. "Is that the girl—— ?"

"Yes. Elizabeth. Nice."

"Nice voice."

"Darling, I was so wrong." Henry's quiet voice had an urgency I had never heard in it, and I turned again to look at them. I saw him touch her hand. "How could I have been so wrong?"

The girl said something I could not hear. After a moment she stretched out her hand and touched his hair.

Mary suddenly straightened and walked sharply back towards the college. I followed her, lighting a cigarette. All sorts of violent little flames were running about in the warm night air: and, if Henry had found his fair girl again, what about red-haired Jenny?

"Happy ending," said Mary shortly, as I caught up with her
"I hope so."
"Show me some more of this nice college."
"Yes, come and look at the tower."
We walked by way of the cloisters to the narrow passage
that runs under the hall into the little quad at the front
pausing in the dark mouth of the passage we looked up at
the great moonlit face of the tower.
"Lovely—— "
"It's rather nice at the top."
"It must be."
"Especially when it's raining. Once, on my birthday, I
went to the top in the rain with a funny little girl I hardly
knew. She borrowed my cap to keep her hair dry. She looked
grotesque. But, do you know, the city was so beautiful in
the rain from up there that I really almost fell in love with
that girl."
"Sweet story."
The small, oddly shaped quad had been empty: but as
Mary spoke a couple walked slowly into the moonlight from
the other end. As they left the deep shadow of the walls for
the chalky whiteness of the grass I recognized Jonathan and
Sarah. My instinct was to call out, or walk and meet them;
but another instinct, unaccountable and unaccountably
strong, made me stay silent in the darkness. Mary did not
move or speak.
"This tower," Jonathan said clearly, "is fantastic inside.
Bell-ropes and ladders and bits of spare sculpture—— "
"Why spare? What a waste."
"Exactly what I always used to feel. Ugly, most of them."
"Is it nice on top?"
"Very nice on top. Some time since I've been on top, of
course, but it used to be very nice indeed. The view's
changed, I expect."

"Bungalows and factories," said Sarah.

"Red brick and tall chimneys."

"What a shame. It must be awful, getting old and see-ing. . . . Oh, I didn't mean," she checked herself. "What a dreadful thing to say."

Jonathan laughed—a perfectly easy laugh. But I was struck, suddenly, by a vivid and savage sense of his vulnera-bility. Elegance he had, charm, success, wealth, popularity; but to this pretty young girl he was old. He could offer everything: but he could not offer what several hundred moist-palmed dancers a few furlongs away took (with some regret) for granted. His plume shook bravely, his armour was shining and perfect; but he had lost his breastplate. Poor Jonathan. Poor old Jonathan. He was entering the lists, a champion, with his arm in a sling. It was unfair. It was gross. And he did not even know the tournament was happening. Did I know? Was the tournament happening? Sue was, in my experience, always right: and I knew that I was always liable to misread situations, failing entirely to see some things and leaping to extravagant conclusions about others. Poor Jonathan? In the mad whiteness of that moon he was being interesting, kind and charming to a pleasant child. He looked extraordinarily handsome. As I knew, none better, he was a man of remarkable perception.

Was I being ridiculous?

Mary, motionless beside me, now coughed a little and moved. We walked out of the doorway into the moon-light.

"Jonathan—— "

"Eddie, how splendid. We were looking at the tower."

"So were we."

"Who's that? Mary, you look lovely."

"Thank you."

"Mary, you haven't danced with me. Which, now I come

to think of it, is probably because I haven't asked you. Will you now?"

"Yes, thank you."

"Oh good. Will you excuse me, Sarah? I'll leave Eddie with you, which will be far nicer for you anyway—— "

"Would you like to dance?" I said to Sarah.

"I *might*—— "

The four of us went back to the big marquee. The crowd was perhaps a little thinner, and the band was certainly playing a more leisurely tune: but it was still far too early in the night for things to have quietened to the level of placidity.

Mary looked at the dance-floor without expression.

"Rather a squash still," said Jonathan. "Never mind. Come on."

"Rather a squash," I said.

"Yes," said Sarah. 'Shall I tell you what I'd like to do?"

"What?"

"Punt. Can we?"

"I expect so. We'll go and see."

"I really wanted to frightfully this afternoon, but Nigel had this party thing he said he had to go to, and we seemed to be such a crowd—— "

"Oh dear, what a pity—— "

"Well, now will be nice."

We crossed the bridge and walked down the path to the wall where the college punts are tied. But there were none. Either the season had, as it were, closed at the end of term, or else other people had had the same idea.

"Oh *boo*."

"I am sorry."

"Never mind. Let's sit on this step for a bit. It's nice here. I'm whacked."

"Not too damp? Not cold?"

"Dry. Warm."

"Good."

We sat quietly looking at the dark water below and the thick leaves all round. Presently a punt whispered under us and clunked against the stone. It was very dark under the trees: I could see only a glimpse of a pale skirt, a hint of faces—two blobs of whiteness, easier to see, like a ship on the horizon, if one looked away.

The blobs, it seemed, swam together and joined. There was a subdued rustle of silk, and then a long, trembling sigh, ending in a small, breathless sob.

"Oh my darling, my darling, darling darling darling—— "

"This is terrible," said a man's whisper.

"I know. I can't help it—— "

"No."

The thin square bow of the punt scraped against the rough stone of the wall, and presently there was a small splash and the punt swam away into even deeper shadow, out of our sight, under the bushes of the other bank.

"Come on," whispered Sarah. "How embarrassing."

We stood up quietly and crept back to the path and along to the bridge.

"Golly," said Sarah, "whoever they are, they're fond of each other. Isn't that nice?"

"Yes," I said.

Evidently she had not recognized the voices from those fragmentary whispers. I had. I knew them both so well.

Chapter Six

✤

I didn't know what to do.

I had a wild idea of surprising them in their punt and so, perhaps, by showing them that all was discovered, of shocking or frightening them out of their catastrophic relationship. But I dismissed this as soon as it occurred to me: I simply could not see myself as a stern-voiced torchholder declaiming about responsibility and loyalty. Tell Jonathan? Too awful. Tell Sue? What good? Do something. Do what?

Sarah and I went slowly back to Nigel's room.

"I'm so touched," she said, "about those two in that punt. I feel like an aunt. Like a fairy god-aunt. Sweet."

"Yes."

"Can you bear to drink any more champagne? I can't. Coffee, now, that's what I'd love."

"I expect Nigel's got some. . . . Yes, here's a percolator. Coffee can you see?"

"Is this?" She sniffed, "yes. *Won*derful"

We filled the percolator and set it on Nigel's electric stove, back-ended in the grate. Sarah prattled charmingly about moonlight, love, punts, Nigel; presently the percolator was bubbling.

"*Won*derful."

Then Christopher and Clare came quietly in.

"Where *have* you been," said Sarah. "You've been missing for hours. Caused talk, I can tell you."

Christopher laughed. "That randy old Major's been gossiping."

"No, not him so much. Me, more."

"That randy young deb."

"That's me."

"Is that coffee I can smell?" said Clare.

"Yes, we found a machine. Look how clever we've been, propping it up like that. Ready soon. Do you want some?"

"Lovely, yes."

"Cups. Has he got any cups?"

"Sure to have."

"Glasses would *do*—— "

"No, cups better. Here."

"Ah yes, huge ones, good. Here we go—isn't it *black*?"

"Lovely."

"Cake?"

"No thanks."

"Clare? Coffee for you?"

"Yes, lovely."

I had to do something.

"Clare," I said, "when we've drunk our coffee, would you like to dance?"

"Well," she said, "the only thing is, I've got rather a headache. I think perhaps—— "

"Oh, I'm sorry—— "

"Headache?" Sue and Tim, at this moment, came laughing through the door. "Poor Clare, have you? Horrid. Is that *coffee*?"

"Yes, have some?"

"Ooh yes, bliss."

"We'll have to make some more," said Sarah. "Fill this, Tim."

"All right."

"Do you want an aspirin, Clare?"

"Oh, no thank you, Sue. I'll be all right if I just sit for a bit.'

"Horrid."

"I'll be all right."

"Bed, do you think?" said Christopher. "Would that be best?"

"Oh no. Not yet. At least, perhaps. Perhaps soon."

"It might be best. Quite late."

"Shall we all go soon?" I said. "Shall I find Jonathan and Mary?"

"No no," said Clare, "don't disturb them. I'll be all right. Coffee will help, so hot, so delicious—— " She sipped, her face expressionless.

"Christopher," I said, "actually, I think we should find Jonathan and Mary."

"Yes, all right. I'll go and look."

"Do. Shall I come?"

"No, stay here. I'll go and look."

As he opened the door Nigel and Caroline came in.

"*Coffee*?"

"Well done," said Nigel, "how bright of you all. Any left?"

"There will be, when we've made some more."

"Are you going, Christopher?"

"Back soon."

"Ah, I see, sorry."

"Not what you think."

Christopher disappeared, and we put the small percolator back on to the stove.

"Sue," I said, "I've got something to show you."

"Show me, darling? What can you mean?"

"Come downstairs a minute."

Tim and Caroline had moved away, over to the far window

again, and were whispering inaudibly. Nigel and Sarah sat close together on the sofa. Clare was lying back, eyes closed, in a big dark armchair.

"All right," said Sue.

A minute later we were standing on the steps below the high colonnade. A black shadow with a hard edge sliced the whiteness of Sue's face. A frond of wistaria leaves nodded over her shoulder.

"Darling, I'm afraid I was right."

"What do you mean?"

"I was right—— "

"Watcher, Maj," said Christopher, appearing suddenly from the gloom, "watcher Sue. No luck."

"What?"

"Couldn't see them anywhere. Canoodling in the shadows, I dare say."

"Oh, that's a pity."

"I don't know. Coming up?"

"In a moment," I said. "We'll follow you."

"We'll come now," said Sue. "Come on, darling."

"But Sue—— "

"Come on."

No one had moved in Nigel's room.

"No good," said Christopher. "Couldn't spot them."

"Did you try the supper-room?"

"Yes, and the bar, and the dance-floor, and round about."

"Pottering somewhere."

"Yes."

"I'm glad," said Clare, "really. We can find them later."

"Aren't we leaving?" I said.

"I don't think *we* are," said Tim, "personally."

"Nor us," said Sarah.

"No, I mean the rest of us. We've got to drive a long, long way to bed. Yours is handy."

"True. Quite, quite true."

"Why don't I drive you home, Clare," said Christopher, "and the others can come later?"

"I think that would be much the best," said Clare, "if you're sure you don't mind?"

"No. I've had enough, really."

"We'll come too," I said.

"No *no*."

"I've had about enough, actually, too—— "

"I haven't," said Sue, "not nearly."

"Good girl," said Christopher. "Don't let the old cowardy-custard run away. Keep him at it. Make him do a Charleston."

"Have a heart," said Sue. "I'm expecting."

"Oh yes, so you are. Well, a tango."

"I don't believe Eddie could be trusted in a tango. I don't believe I could, really—— "

"If you're going," I said, "we must tell Jonathan."

"No no," said Clare, "he'd be worried and want to leave —I don't want to spoil his evening."

"Is Mary staying at Fordings?" Sue asked.

"Yes. So Jonathan can bring her."

"We don't want to spoil her evening," I said.

"No, *exactly*."

"I think, perhaps," I said, "back in a moment—— " I left quickly and ran down the stairs. Christophe and Clare were going to have two hours, perhaps, alone ogether at Fordings before the rest of us trailed back. I ad to find Jonathan.

I scudded round the edge of the still-full floor (they were now swaying, all of them, to something very new and very slow) searching frantically for Jonathan's silver head and Mary's neat dark head. I tried the bar tent. I ran, jostling gay parties and slow-stepping, quiet couples, down the cloisters to the hall stairs, and looked hurriedly up and down the supper-tables. I tried the bridge. Coming away, back towards the dance-floor, I saw them. They were a good way off, walking briskly as though about to dance.

"Jonathan!"

"Eddie!" I stopped and turned. "Eddie!" It was Henry Fenwick, beaming, with the thin, fair girl called Elizabeth. "Eddie, come and have a drink."

"Oh, Henry, hullo—I can't just now—give me a second."

"No, do," said the fair girl, and suddenly laughed with great happiness.

"Give me just a moment—— "

I ran to the door of the marquee: but the check had been just too long. Jonathan and Mary had disappeared. Miserably I watched the swinging brilliance of the dancers—it was a waltz again—in the certainty that they were not among them. They had gone through. They might be anywhere in the dark acres of the college: in any room: in any crowd.

"Eddie, don't dash about like that. Come and have a drink."

"Yes," I said heavily, "sorry. I had to catch—I tried to catch—— "

"Catch her later. Do you know Elizabeth? Darling, this is Eddie Melot."

"How do you do?" she said. Her voice was enchanting, as I had thought on the bridge. "I've heard of you, I think, from Lavinia and those people."

"Lavinia? Yes, you might have. Do you know them?"

"Plainly she does," said Henry, "damn it."

"Yes, of course. Stupid question."

"As who doesn't?" he went on, "as who doesn't?"

"Do you like them, that lot?" asked Elizabeth.

"Well," I said carefully, "they're intelligent, aren't they? and—— "

She laughed again, with charming, total, irrelevant delight.

"Do I gather—— ?" I said.

"Yes."

"Oh—congratulations."

"Thank you," said Henry. "Come on. We're using someone's rooms over here—— "

They led me back into the cloisters and up a staircase. It was a big room, well-lit, crowded. Jeremy and Clarissa Laxton stood by the fireplace; Angelica and the fair-haired man with the spot sat on a sofa; one of the men I had seen Elizabeth dining with, now drunk, sat glumly in a window; other, strange figures were gaily grouped about drinking and talking. Jenny was not, I think, there.

They all crowded round Henry and Elizabeth, congratulating them (they all seemed to know the story: where, I wondered, was Jenny?) and someone poured us out some champagne. I chatted, I hope politely, to Elizabeth and a small girl in a red dress and a man in spectacles: and I felt hopelessness come down over me like an infinite eiderdown. Things were out of control. What could I do? Presently I left, cheerily (I hope) saying good-bye to them all and thanking them for the champagne: and stood a moment later, undecided, in the crossword-puzzle shadows of the cloisters. What could I do? I walked quickly to the dance-floor and looked, without any hope, briefly over the crowd. Then I walked slowly back to Nigel's staircase and up to his room.

Tim and Caroline were still sitting together in the far window. Nigel and Sarah had disappeared—I thought I remembered noticing them on the dance-floor, moving very slowly. Sue was where Clare had been, leaning comfortably back in the big shabby chair.

"Have they gone?"

"Who?" said Sue, "Christopher and Clare?"

"Yes."

"She had a headache," said Sue unnecessarily. "Yes, they've gone."

"Oh God," I said, quietly so that the others by the windows should not hear. "Oh God, how awful."

Tim and Caroline got up; arm in arm, smiling, they walked slowly to the door and left without a word.

"Sue—— "

"I know."

"I was right."

"Of course you were right. I knew you were right."

"Then why—— ?"

"In the punt I knew. And at dinner. Poor Mary. . . . But still, you can't go wading in."

"What? I must find Jonathan."

"No."

"Sue, I must. Jonathan is—I owe Jonathan nearly everything. I must find him."

"Oh darling, no."

I looked at her, not understanding.

"I frightfully don't want to leave," she said.

"But. . . . Are you sure you're not tired yourself?"

"Not a bit tired. Do let's stay. Don't worry."

"Don't *worry*—— "

"Or interfere. Just stay, and we'll enjoy ourselves." She looked up at me. "Just stay here quietly."

But I got up and went out and down the stairs again. Poor Jonathan.

I saw him almost at once. They were coming away from the ha-ha by the deer park. I heard Mary's laugh—she sounded more cheerful than she had all evening.

"Jonathan!"

"Eddie, hullo. Why are you walking about all by yourself? Have you no wives?"

"I was looking for you. Clare—— "

"Yes?"

"She's got a headache. We tried to find you. She and Christopher have gone home."

"Oh—poor sweet."

"Poor thing," said Mary, in an oddly muffled voice.

"Yes."

"In that case," said Jonathan, "and given the lateness of the hour, I think, don't you, we might all be going home?"

"Yes, I agree. Sue says she wants to stay, but she's looking a bit tired—— "

"Ah yes. Persuade her away, I should."

"That's what I feel."

"What about you, Mary? We've got quite a drive—— "

"Yes, any time."

"Good. We'll go and find Nigel—— "

"I doubt if you will," I said, "or even if he'd want to be found."

"No, there's that. Better not, perhaps."

"Let's just slide away."

"I daresay you're right. Coats we need, and Sue we need. Where's your car, Eddie?"

"Longwall."

"And mine."

We collected Sue, and Mary's white coat, and walked round by the main lodge to Longwall Street. Sue was very silent.

Then, when I tried to start my car, I found nothing would happen.

"My dear Eddie," said Jonathan, "what a bore."

"It'll start on the handle."

But it didn't.

"The battery's stone dead. How odd—— "

"You've got petrol?"

"Yes, it's the battery. Or the pump or the ignition or something. I don't see how we can cope now—— "

"Would you consider leaving it and coping by telephone tomorrow?"

"And coming with you? I would indeed, yes. It'll be all right here."

"Perfectly all right."

"No one can pinch it," said Sue, "if it won't go."

"True. Hop in—— "

As we purred out of Oxford towards the downs and Newbury, I put my arm round Sue's soft shoulder: but she shrugged away and huddled down in the corner.

"Tired, darling?"

"No."

"Then. . . ."

"Why did you do it?" she whispered fiercely, "what have you done?"

"I had to, darling. Jonathan—— "

She looked at me as though I were a stranger. "What have you done?"

"But Sue—— "

She turned away and stared out of her window at the brightening east.

"Extraordinary thing," said Jonathan, "Clare's not here."

We were standing in the thick-carpeted upstairs hall at Fordings. Mary and Sue were downstairs, making hot drinks in the kitchen at Jonathan's suggestion; I had been carrying Sue's and my suitcases up to our room, and Jonathan had immediately gone to see Clare.

"Is Christopher's car in the garage?" I asked.

"Come to think of it, I didn't notice. I'll go and look. God, I hope they haven't broken down, I expect Clare's pretty tired—— "

Christopher's car, low and sleek, was in the garage, edged neatly against the far side.

"Extraordinary thing, where can she be? I can't have made a mistake, can I?"

We went in again by the back door. As we passed the kitchen Sue called out: "Ready. Don't let it get cold."

"Just a moment, Sue," said Jonathan.

"You *must* drink it now, it'll be beastly when it gets cold."

As we climbed the back stairs we came opposite the door of the small room Christopher always used at For dings. A thin line of light showed at the bottom.

"Christopher's here, anyway—— "

Jonathan knocked and opened the door. Feeling a weight like a flat-iron in the pit of my stomach I followed him into the room. The bedside lamp was on, casting a pool of golden light over the broad pillows. Christopher and Clare, locked together fair head by fair head, looked up at us with wide, blank eyes. A leather-covered clock on the bedside table ticked deafeningly. Clare released a long, shuddering breath, never taking her eyes off Jonathan. The covers were pushed down to their waists. Naked, she looked soft and very beautiful in that soft gold light. Christopher's face was frozen: staring. I could not look at Jonathan. We were all four silent and motionless for a long time.

PART FOUR

Liebestod

Liebestod

✣

Jonathan, putting forth an effort I could almost feel, turned quickly and left the room. I followed, shutting the door quietly. In the narrow, softly lit passage he stopped and faced me. I could not see his face clearly—the light was behind him; I have no idea what expression his features wore.

"Good night, Eddie," he said gravely. "Sleep well."

I made some kind of noise in the back of my throat and turned and walked heavily down the passage and along to my room. When I had my hand on the doorknob I remembered Mary and Sue and the hot drinks in the kitchen: so I went downstairs.

"It's getting cold," said Sue. "Where's Jonathan?"

"He's found Clare,"

"Yes, I suppose so."

She put down her cup with a rattle and stood looking at me. "What have you done?"

Then she picked up her little silver bag and walked out of the kitchen without looking at me again.

"Have some," said Mary. "It's hot still.'"

"What?"

"You might as well," she said gently, "now it's made. It's hot."

"Oh—yes. Thank you,"

She poured whatever it was out of a saucepan, into a big cup and handed it to me. "What's going to happen?"

"I don't know." Then I said: "What else could I have done?"

She looked up at me from the high stool by the stove. "I don't know."

Presently I went upstairs again and into our bedroom. Sue was sitting on the arm of a chair by the window, her back to me, motionless. She had started to undress, but had not got very far. The window was wide open. There was no movement of air, and the curtains and her soft hair hung perfectly still.

I walked over to her.

The dawn was far advanced now. The noise of the birds was subsiding as the world whitened, and there were broad strips of yellow in the east, over to our left, and clear grey above. The high trees beyond the walled garden lifted their heads out of a low bank of white mist. On the far side of the shallow valley the smoke of an early train hung motionless in the pale air. On the broad lawn below our window, over the wet gleam of a heavy dew, long faint shadows, grey over grey, ran already from left to right.

Jonathan was walking slowly across the lawn towards the border by the tennis court at the end. His hands were in his trouser pockets. He was in his tail coat still, without an overcoat, and his grey hair was still perfectly brushed. He walked erect, with deliberation, steadily. At the border he turned and walked slowly back, and then again turned, into the eye of the dawn, towards the border.

I began to feel old and cold.

I put my hand on Sue's bare shoulder. "You'll catch cold."

She seemed not to notice.

"What could I have done, Sue? What else could I have done?"

She seemed not to notice.

I came down at ten after a miserable night. Sue had got up much earlier and had dressed and gone down without a word; when I came into the morning-room only Clare was there, very pale, in a grey print dress.

"Has everyone gone?"

"Yes," she said.

"Jonathan?"

"He left hours ago. An hour ago. He took Sue and Mary."

"Christopher?"

"He left before that. Hours ago."

"Are you staying?"

"No."

"Shall I drive you up?"

"All right."

Presently I put my suitcase, Sue's, and three of Clare's into the car. We had a slow, tiresome drive to London in heavy Saturday traffic. Clare never spoke, but stared, as though sightlessly, at the road ahead. When I spoke to her she looked at me, if she did, as though I were not only a complete stranger, but also a foreigner speaking some language she did not know.

None too soon we got to Eaton Square and their flat.

"Is this right?"

Clare got out and I began to pull the suitcases out of the back seat.

"Leave them."

"All right."

She let herself into the front door and walked towards the lift. I hung back, not knowing what to do.

"Come on," she said.

"Oh—all right."

We took the lift to the third floor. In the bronued, many-mirrored baroque of the lift I felt a curious association with Clare, quite surprising to me. I touched her arm and said: "I'm sorry."

She looked at me with a very small smile in her tired face. "That's all right."

"What are you going to do, Clare?"

Before she answered the lift stopped and I opened the two doors and let her go ahead of me out of the lift. We crossed the passage and she unlocked the door of the flat.

"Come on," she gestured me in.

"Thank you—— " I couldn't understand why she wanted me in; or what she was going to do; or what this was all about.

"What are you going to do?" I said again.

She sat down, suddenly, in the chair by the telephone-table in that shiny attractive hall. She looked terribly tired: pale, bruised almost, helpless.

"I don't know."

A pile of letters lay by the telephone. I turned them over, absently, awkwardly. Most were the yellowish or buff envelopes of official correspondence, or had the cellophane windows of bills or receipts. One, in a big manilla envelope, lay a little apart from the others. It said "Clare" in Jonathan's writing.

"Here."

"Oh—— "

Her fingers shook a little as they opened the envelope, but her face had no expression at all. As she drew out a single sheet and unfolded it I watched her curiously.

As she read, something happened to her face. Her eyes widened a little. The flesh round the sides of her mouth tautened. The soft muscles in her temples and jaw stood out. Her tiredness vanished. Colour flooded her face from hair-line to throat. She looked as though she wanted to shout, or perhaps scream.

Still I stood quiet.

"Jonathan— " she began, and stopped.

Still I could not tell if this were bad news or good: if this were a rush of anger, jubilation, defeat, victory, death, life.

"Jonathan's dead."

She handed me the letter. It was quite short:

Clare, perhaps I was wrong to marry you, perhaps you were wrong to marry me, perhaps this was bound to happen. I don't know what I can do about anything, except go. In any case I'm not much interested in the prospect of trying to live without you. Everything goes to Christopher, so you'll be all right. I hope you'll be happy. All my love, always. Mag.

"Mag?"

"Yes, I called him Mag," she murmured.

I looked up from the terrible little letter to her face.

"I called him Mag. It was a joke we had. It was short for magnate. Just a joke— "

But she was not thinking of Jonathan much; she was not much aware of me. Her eyes, bright now and looking over my head at the wall, were seeing (I thought) the beginning of a new life, a life with Christopher: life, love, victory. There was something rapt in her face. She was more beautiful, in that moment, than I had ever seen her.

Out of death life, I thought. Out of sacrifice happiness. Out of that moment of shattering horror and shock this rebirth, this beauty.

"Shall I take you to Chelsea?"

She dragged herself back to the hall and my words. "What?"

"Shall I drive you to Flood Street?"

"Will you? Thank you— "

So we went out and down again and drove to   Christopher's flat, her three suitcases still in the back of the car.

The morning was magnificent. The trees in Sloane Square

had the eternal look of things powerful and still growing; the swarming shoppers in the King's Road had a holiday air, as though everything in their string-bags were for treats or birthdays; as we turned left down Flood Street a very small girl paused on the pavement and waved us on with the portentousness of a traffic policeman.

My own mood was quite negative. These events had not yet registered. The tooth, was out: the jaw was still numb.

As we drew up outside Christopher's flat the click of my handbrake seemed to trigger Clare to action. She opened her door and ran across the pavement and up the steps and rang the bell and then knocked with all the happy violence of a child.

I sat still, watching.

After a moment Clare rang again, holding the bell-push down for long seconds. Presently the door opened. As Clare started quickly in, a comfortable, slippered figure appeared. I could not hear what they said: but I saw the old lady in the slippers give Clare a letter, smile, nod, smile again, and shut the door. Clare, alone on the step, stared for a long time at the envelope, then slowly tore it open and read the letter.

The gay London sun beat down on that red step. A boy on a bicycle, whistling shrilly, swung in crazy loops past me and down towards the Embankment. A sparrow fluttered down on to the paving stones of the little yard in front of the house and hopped about in purposeless zigzags, cocking a mad, knowing eye at the car. Horns tooted and life went on in the King's Road, a hundred yards behind us: but Clare stood, motionless, staring at the letter.

When at last she came back to the car, she opened the door and got in without a word.

"Eaton Square?"

"Yes," she whispered.

"Gone?"

"Yes. America."

There was no more to be said.

I drove back to Eaton Square concentrating entirely on the road; and when we had stopped once again outside the house I could not look at her tragic face.

Again we took the lift (why did I feel this odd association with Clare—this identity, almost—among those ornate mirrors, in the hiss and thud of that lift?) and again she gestured me into the flat. She led the way along the hall and opened the door at the end: the drawing-room. She went on into the room and then, a yard from the door, stopped dead. Coming up behind her, looking over her shoulder, I saw Jonathan sitting upright, half-smiling, in a chair by the fireplace.

"Hullo Clare," he said, "hullo Eddie."

Neither of us spoke or moved.

His smile was a little crooked and he looked down at his shoes. "Take that note as unwritten. I decided not to do it." He looked up again. He was as perfectly groomed as always —hair ordered, tie straight, coat well brushed. "Also, Christopher left me a message at the office about his plans."

He got up and came over to Clare. Instinctively I backed towards the door.

"Don't go, Eddie," he glanced at me gently. "It was kind of you to chauffeur Clare."

He took Clare's hand and led her to a chair and let her sink down into it. "Sorry to give you such a shock, darling. Have you got your bags?"

"In the car," I said. "Shall I—— ?"

"That would be kind, Eddie, yes. Thank you so much."

So I got the suitcases (making two trips from the car to the lift and two from the lift to the flat) and piled them in the hall.

"Thank you so much, that is kind-

Clare spoke at last: "Would we all like some coffee?"

"Yes, darling, I think coffee would be delicious, don't you Eddie?"

"Delicious—— "

"All right—— "

So the three of us sat sipping coffee in that big, bright drawing-room, and Jonathan and I discussed Belgravia Bond and Mr. Robinson's zip-fasteners and the meetings we were to have the following week: and after half-an-hour I got up to go.

The mirrors in the lift were a little out of truth. Staring at myself on the way down I saw a squatter, squarer man than I was used to. I stood on tip-toe and became thin-faced and sly. I bent my knees and became Eskimo.

Later, talking to Sue, I became almost myself again: almost the man I was used to.